**Ice Age**

Winner of the Flannery O'Connor Award for Short Fiction

**Ice Age**  Stories by Robert Anderson

The University of Georgia Press  Athens and London

Published by the University of Georgia Press
Athens, Georgia 30602
© 2000 by Robert Anderson

Designed by Erin Kirk New
Set in 10/13 Berkeley by G&S Typesetters
Printed and bound by Maple-Vail

The paper in this book meets the guidelines for
permanence and durability of the Committee on
Production Guidelines for Book Longevity of the
Council on Library Resources.

Printed in the United States of America
04   03   02   01   00   C   5   4   3   2   1

Library of Congress Cataloging-in-Publication Data

Anderson, Robert, 1964–
   Ice age : stories/by Robert Anderson.
      p. cm.
   "Winner of the Flannery O'Connor Award for short fiction"—
   P. preceding t.p.
   ISBN 0-8203-2243-1 (alk. paper)
      I. Title.
   PS3551.N3796 I28 2000
   813'.6—dc21                00-029901

British Library Cataloging-in-Publication Data available

"Schism" first appeared in *The Iowa Review*

"Death and the Maid" first appeared in *American Writing: A Magazine*

In memoriam:

Eva Anderson

and

Jean Persaud

**Contents**

# Ice Age

**Mother Tongue**   Cause was cure. Of course, hair of dog, right? The proposition touched a cold mallet to his forehead and dropped the trip-hammer proper into Mailer's lap. Cause-effect-cure was no warring triumvirate, no irreconcilable holy trinity, and no algebraic tribulation after all. It made sense only as a syllogism, variable A and variable C sharing a common identity. You heard about cause endlessly—additives, pesticides, saturated fats, carbon monoxide, socialism, television, nuclear physics, Forty-second Street, Jerry Lee Lewis, Mickey Spillane—and effect was there for everyone to see, but where was the data on cure? The good preached prayer and abstinence just as they had done in the Dark Ages and the bad preached theater, bidding us all to become actors of the moment, as they did during the

Renaissance. Cause was cure; therefore cure could kill cause. Speaking of Dark Ages, why was he only now realizing something he'd known all along?

At least he always acted like he knew. Hadn't he taken courtesans in rooms off the Boulevard Des Invalides, disdaining the hypocrisy of the tickler? Hadn't he dueled with Jap artillerymen, exposed on a bluff, across a river boiling with lead? Had he not called Eisenhower a woman on Mike Wallace's *Night Beat*? You wanna talk living dangerously? He was going on Wallace again this coming Sunday—how astonished the viewers would be to learn that the Great Cure was the Siamese twin of the Great Cause and that the two procreated by merely standing sideways, and thus creating a crowd of onlookers.

Whoa, make a note of that; link voyeurism with politics, both of them being lonely, haphazard, and vaguely effeminate means to an end—orgasm, however derived, and elected office were one and the same from a literary standpoint since both of them held something of the finality of death. Way off the topic now, though.

"Mike, I'm running for mayor for my own damn good reasons, to cure my own damn good cancer. God knows the electorate doesn't need me except that they need me in the sense that they deserve me. They read me, don't they? . . . Well, they read *Advertisements* so that they could send irate letters to G. P. Putnam's Sons and stage whisper the sexy bits around the cooler and under the dryer. 'Overly stylized,' said the *Washington Post*. 'Hipapocalypse,' said *Life* magazine. 'Yikes,' said Mr. and Mrs. Willie Winnebago. So, what can I do to get your vote, Mike? You want a date with Lillian Hellman? You guys could browbeat each other until she gets an ectopic pregnancy on her forehead. You know, 'Congratulations, the two of you are mother and father to a fine and healthy carbuncle.' Okay, we're going to break now so that Mike can sell you some more crockery. The soup bowl makes a great pith helmet at parties. 'Hooray for Captain Spalding, the African explorer . . . '"

Maybe this mayoralty thing wasn't such a hot idea at that.

Oh yes it was, he thought as he was waking the next morning, the steaming coffee cup forming a devil's stovepipe in the pillow, the maid's proficient little steel-to-steel and steel-to-enamel noises coming in from the kitchen, and Adele Morales Mailer chattering like a happy kid, her visceral springs fully recoiled from the ten hours of lazy slut sleep she must have gotten while he brooded through the night over their redemption. The girls would be at dance or dramatics or at the neighbors' down on Ninety-second. Whose redemption? His redemption. He must learn to leave out this "they" and "their" business. Once there was an external fugue as well as an internal fugue and the two blended beyond the best hopes of algebra, but then tonic and dominant turned to barking and bickering on one or other and then both sides of the fence. Take it like a solo act, Norman. You could be the most self-contained man on earth. Look at you now, lying in bed, stewing your own guts like cabbage and getting the giddiest little kick out of the glower of your curdled bourbon and marijuana breath as it blasts back at you from the coffee cup. Well, Madame Adele talked to her gin glass, didn't she? He lost count of how many times he'd overheard her. She confided in it like a wishing well. For the rest of his life, he must abstain from gin—it knew him too well. His mistress over on the East Side— a bona fide British Ladyship—drank only white rum.

Would the syllogism hold up under a hangover? "Let's see what it's made of," Mailer garbled to himself. The disease and the vaccine hold the seeds of each other in their bellies and effect is but the marrying agent, the wizened votary who bids them to kiss. Vaccine—tincture of orange mold, snake oil, omega-blocker, male—kills disease—karmic equalizer, germ of death and enlightenment, female—through the process of melding, through a copulation as ordained and incestuous as Adam and Eve's, but only if he is so worthy as to bring her to an internal simmer, to break up those woven and enigmatic compounds which have defied lab work and definition through the ages. Here is the world made whole in the same petri dish that spawned the hydrogen bomb of *The Naked and the Dead*.

Good show. How ridiculous. How authoritative. Let Mailer tell you something about truth. Verisimilitude is verisimilitude relative to its concealment. The blue sky has validity only to the blind and truth is like an alarm clock, someone else's alarm clock in another room and only when you've overslept. Mailer looked up from his coffee and said to nobody, "It's the man with all the answers that has the most to learn. That's why I'm running for mayor."

---

Adele came into the bedroom. Her features were unusually aligned for this hour of the morning and her eyes projected the bright, hard gauntlet of the East Harlem double Dutch champ she never was outside of Norman's wish fulfillment. Some Perry Street apothecary—would they ever succeed in moving far enough away from the Village?—brewed her an herbal purgative with a handicapped kick like a spinster's eggnog (yes, Norman sipped some) and she drank it last night in lieu of her usual martini intake. Eureka, this morning her features had all the glow of a spic-and-span colon.

"You got the last of the milk, baby. I don't have any for tea with Lucas and he'll be here any minute."

Lucas was Lucas Swafford, Adele's art coach and onetime drinking buddy of Jackson Pollock, he said, who gave liquor up for good when they found bad time Charlie in a tree alongside the road to East Hampton. He wasn't competition; far from it, fiftyish Lucas had the wispy coxcomb and the slackened neck common, it seemed, to all those older art types who once knew someone seminal. If he couldn't cadge whiskey off of an apocryphal association, he'd go for tea.

"Couldn't Lyris go?" Mailer asked.

"Lyris is fixing your lunch?"

"Lunch?"

"Two P.M., baby."

There it is. The clock of truth. It tolls even for Norman.

"You gonna go for the milk?"

"Why can't you make me lunch?"

"Lyris—"

"I didn't marry Lyris, did I?"

"You'd screw her if you could."

And he laughed. Lyris was in her sixties and had a complexion that presaged her corpse. When she smiled, her crow's-feet reminded him of a batter digging in at the plate.

"Forget it, I'll run and get the milk," Adele said. "Put some clothes on and entertain Lucas if he comes."

"I thought I was gonna screw Lyris."

"Hush, not so loud, Norman."

"Hey, Adele."

She turned back into the doorway. He liked that look over her shoulder. One great dark Peruvian eye frescoed above the bulb of her cheek.

"I love you."

"Tell it to the *Times*," she sneered.

He laughed again. The marriage was on the ropes, sure, but it still had its reflexes. "Tell it to the *Times*" was a running gag they'd kept up for years. Long ago, in his naiveté, he would phone a certain *Times* columnist to lend a bon mot now and again. The guy would thank him cordially and then spite him with utter neglect in print. Norman thought that the columnist was currently collecting his pension and stringing in chess stratagems and soufflé recipes. God, he felt good. Party tonight.

———

This was nice; to be in the root bed of the house, alone and with the phone lines silent, his own wires extending into the various antechambers. This went back to his heritage of the temple. The Patriarch's house was the bellwether of the universe, and this was a part of himself that Mailer acknowledged less and less these days. Let Malamud mine the Jewish neurosis, the Jew love-hated himself while the good Christian love-hated his God. Who'd hooked the bigger fish? The girls were back and watching laugh track TV—don't get him started—in their bedroom, and Lucas Swafford and Adele were in the studio chatting, Adele, now and then, floor scraping out another of her canvases to illustrate the latest mediocrity to come up in conversation. Lucas's voice was a virus of the Golden State. (This was something he also thought the Negroes picked up with an alacrity propelled by media. In a decade, they'd gone from Kingfish to king-of-arms.) As with so many West Coasters, Lucas's accent was a variation on that of the early hour jazz DJ who utters "Brewbeck" with a stuttered lick like brush against drum hide. He was saying, "You turn it on by turning all else off. It's the very last switch. Like, what do you see before you sleep?"

"The back of Norman's shoulder. When he's home."

"C'mon, Adele, what have I been telling you? You gotta leave Norman out of it."

Oh, yeah? With that Adele got up and went to the turntable and dropped the *Toccata and Fugue in D Minor* to serve as her and Lucas's little communion antiphon. He didn't think he'd ever discussed the gloomy masterpiece with Adele, but he had to grant her access to the master controls of his nervous system, else what would be the point of the marriage? He finds something horribly martial in the fabric of the piece, some great, rhapsodic belligerence, something like Sgt. Croft's "Recon, up!" or Sergius O'Shaughnessy's command of "All rise" to his own genitals. This was not the hour for the *Toccata* and Adele wasn't leaving Norman out of it at all. He could tell her to turn it off; it was his house, wasn't it? But he would need her for tonight. She could either be a captivating hostess, or she could curl against the wallpaper with a drink in her hand and regard the guests in the same way the captive panther, tethered to a painted jungle backdrop, looks at zoo guests. "Oh, if you and I were only in the wild," Adele's eyes would be saying.

He wanted to write, but he was in exile from fiction until he could come up with something resistant to the Zippos of the critics, and for two months of trying, his agent hadn't hooked a decent journalism assignment. The alternate escape hatch was the fine alchemy of bourbon and pot, but the liquor and the makings were in the kitchen cupboard—Lyris was always complaining that the "mildew" smell of the grass undercut the empyrean of her floor wax. He would have to pass Adele's studio. Well, what of it? The worst they could do would be to ask his opinion.

Adele had her blinds up and the withering fluorescence of the afternoon lent a great deal to the Rothkoesque block of vermilion that she and Lucas were looking at. They turned their heads as he passed and he said, "Getting to the bottom of it?" half under his breath.

"It has no bottom, Norman," Lucas said. And this was true, Abstract art was dimensionless and redeemed largely by its coupling with Zen, albeit the association was ex post facto in nature and brokered entirely by famished critics. But he'd crossed into the kitchen now and the current of ammonia coming off of the floor tiles tingled up into his ankles. He felt a benignity toward the art form. It was based on simple sensation rather than observation and, who knows, this sensory god/fraud might yet amount to a wondrous prodigy, only now learning to play his scales.

"Nor-man, you're not getting high already, are you?" Adele called from the studio as the *Toccata*'s final measures ricocheted around the walls and Mailer, without even having lit the snout of the dragon yet, heard a sound picture that delighted him to no end—a squadron of Texas lariat wizards winding up for the moon.

"I'm not gettin' high, I'm aimin' high!" he hollered back in his best cowboy accent.

---

At the price of eleven pesos, the bullfighter's shirt was from God, the gawking sun god who scorched the Mexican earth and endowed the flora that happened to survive its eye with a shapely green luxuriance as totemic as flames—*mirada fuerte* indeed—and Norman loved the shirt all the more for the fact that the material was as hot as stove mitts when he first plucked it from the pile in the clothing stall. The air pocket shoulders, the wilting accordion front, the primitive jailhouse shivs embroidered on either breast—the shirt said "death" and it said "grace," and it said that both were children of the heat. He was going to wear it to the party and Adele had put on a low-cut black crepe number, her breasts worked up into a pearly armature. He could hear the girls, already in bed, whispering in lower and lower tones, their vicarious excitement counting them down to oblivion as deftly as a lullaby.

"You invite anybody?" he said to Adele and she looked over at him, disbelieving that he would breach the hush of the dressing ritual—both of them tended to preen like prom kids, never exchanging a word.

"Lucas. And he's not coming."

"That's it?"

"The way you canvassed, we're going to have to use Riverside Park as an annex as it is."

"I tried to get Eleanor this afternoon," he said, and she left it hanging. As always, he felt a fist closing in his belly.

"I—"

"Who's Eleanor?"

"Roosevelt."

"You're kidding?"

"No. I called that hotel in D.C. You know, the ladies' residence she stays at."

"Still?"

"Yes, but she's in West Virginia. There's been a mine collapse."

"What's she gonna do about it?"

"They take her by the heels and use her for a divining rod. When she starts to froth at the mouth—"

"Okay, Norman."

Mailer said, "I didn't mean that she was ugly. It's just her overwrought sense of caring. She's born rich, you know, and—"

"I didn't say anything about ugly either," Adele said.

"I think she has a face of antiquity."

"Then or now?"

He hated it that he couldn't laugh. Her attitude and all.

"Funny. I called Hyannisport. The compound," he said.

"Oh, God."

"No, oh, Jack."

"You get him?"

"No, I got a kid. A nephew. 'Uncle Jack's in Miami with Grandpa Joe.'"

"What do you think they're talking about, Norman?"

"The future. God forbid either of them should talk about their pasts. I really wanted Jack here tonight."

"Superman comes to the super-manhole," Adele said. Christ, her mind was quick sometimes.

"You know, Adele, I think art will inform this decade more than politics. Corporations, you see, will need a more highbrow opiate as the country grows more affluent. Especially the television networks. Then, you just watch. The biggest backfire since—"

"So, you tell them, Norman. What do you need Jack Kennedy for?"

"Yeah, you're right. Anyway, I got through to Plimpton and he's bringing in the brain trust. Adele, I noticed that you're not drinking."

"Party's not started yet, baby."

---

He waited out the preliminaries in the bedroom. The early guests all commented on how great Adele looked (would they use the adjective "ravishing" if he were in the room?) and named their drinks, some of them saying, "I'll get it myself, hon," remembering from former parties her ineptitude as a chemist. "Where is Norman?" or "Where's Daddy-o?" or even "Where's your more prodigious half?" reverberated around the room, and Adele— bless her—played it off with "He had a very important root canal to go to," and "He's in a bubble bath with our otter." "Be patient," she told them. Then the party noises became cacophonous and through the wall he could feel the density of the room—afternoons in Flatbush so long ago, Norman biking by Ebbets Field. The pagan bleacher chorus would be calling for blood and there was even an unschooled brass band in those days to nettle the nerves of the opposing team ("the Bums" had long ago grown immune). Mailer, at eleven, twelve, and thirteen, thought of the troubled sleep of Jehovah and kept his prayers as concise as postcards.

He was holding up well, considering that he'd trained for the party by boozing and toking for three days straight. He moved about the bedroom, danced in place, and his bloodstream sang of mercury like a chiming cathedral bell. The trouble was in his tongue. The pot dehydrated it and the bourbon lent it thickness. He had this problem last night and he'd gone to the bathroom and licked the running faucet. No chance of that now. The best he could do was to try a declamatory exercise so he turned to the wall and offered the first Shakespearean disquisition that came to mind. "This by summer's ripening breath" came out "Dis by dummer's ripening blath." He hit the offending member with a fresh slug of bourbon and spat on the carpet. The scales fell away. "Ladies and gentleman," he said in a suitably patrician Harvard voice, self-cured by self-cause, "the next mayor of the city of New York, No Man Mauler," and he gave himself a round. He opened the bedroom door and the single peacock of over a hundred guests—bank panicked out into the hallway and down the stairwell—turned and fanned him and countless starry eyes inquired of his sanity. Startled, he looked away and directly into the bedroom mirror. He was wearing a bullfighter's shirt and holding a half-empty bourbon bottle, his dark hair (hadn't he just combed it?) springing up like a pommeled crown.

"Fetes and trumpets," he shouted. He listened to the laughter and didn't hear Adele's.

———

Once he was out of the bedroom, there was a round of gladhanding and a couple of bear hugs and Tony Franciosa, television detective or whatever, waved from the divan where the ladies of the gathering were taking orderly shifts sitting on either side of him. He couldn't hear a word of what they were saying, but he guessed that the topics might be Tony's suntan and Tony's dental work. After a few moments, Tony even looked over and almost nodded as though he'd cat-burgled his way onto Norman's wavelength. Mailer elbowed through the room in a hurry to stop

Allen Ginsberg from avenging Norman Podhoretz's opinion of Jack Kerouac. He took Ginsberg by the wrist and gentled him away from Podhoretz, and Allen gave him a look that he was most familiar with on the faces of shamed dogs.

"Allen," he said, "you're a poet. You'd better leave the fisticuffs to guys like me."

"You are not a poet?" Allen asked.

"Hell, no, I'm a writer."

His tongue stiffened up again and an angel of dissipation came and sat on his cranium—he could feel the split of her anus cutting a seam across his skull, her wide, liquid thighs a lodestone around his shoulders. No Jack, no Eleanor, and him with this bitch on his back; the party had gone rudderless and was drifting in circles along the shallows. Where was the Plimpton-promised intelligentsia? He wasn't sure whom this intelligentsia might consist of, but a promise was a promise. For that matter, where the hell was George Plimpton? C. Wright Mills holding forth beneath the bookshelves. "Crooked commie dew-heart philosopher," the Texas patrolman who resided, once in a while, in his mind said. If Mills had a tan and capped teeth, he'd talk them up in place of Trotsky. Maybe he should buttonhole Ginsberg. Would Ginsberg be willing to announce his candidacy for him? Would he tell the guests that they could cure their cancers by reveling in them? Would he sit on Norman's lap and let Norman turn his knobs? No way he would. For starters, Norman wasn't unwashed enough. So, what about Adele? Adele was talking to a woman, good. She was doing all right on the turntable, too—Sun Ra and Sonny Rollins and it was no accident that the nebula of blue-tinged cigarette smoke had settled directly over the stereo. But would Adele be willing to clap the party to attention and then say, "My husband is running for mayor and he'd like you to know that the excess of the soul is also the health of the soul, employed with the proper discretion, of course?" Would she say, "The Zeitgeist is running wild, go and chase it for dear life?"

Adele was standing next to a brown-skinned woman with diamond-clear cat eyes and a black drum of hair and the two of them were racing along the speedway of the Spanish language, their hand gestures serving as auxiliary units of communication and the two of them were absolutely in sync, like two kids playing shadow. Each time Mailer glanced, they seemed to have moved a millimeter closer—did they want to verify the suspicion of kinship in the scent of each other's breath? Casually, they backed into the bathroom together and he caught Adele's index finger straying from the bulb of her gin glass just long enough to draw the door closed. Well, women did that and they did that purely for aesthetic reasons, they compared stockings and underthings, and bolstered each other's cleavages; it was merely a retention of the psychology of the doll keeper, that prettified bridge to womanhood.

He listened for giggles from behind the door, but then Sonny Rollins hit a squall out on the high seas and Ginsberg, recovered now, was talking much too loud about Pound. The name Pound put Norman in mind of Atlas. Yes, he would like to hear of Atlas and the ease the eyes of the Gorgon brought to him as he trembled under the weight of the heavens and earth instead of Ezra Pound, who wasn't so much a traitor to his country but a traitor to his own salvation—that taut centurion rope of sanity. In the end, one went mad on purpose; you might well be pushed to the brink, but never past it. He resolved to phone his mistress. She was the circuit breaker for situations like this. Adele and Lady Jeanne had never met, thank fate, but they existed in parallel universes. Adele lit a cigarette; Lady Jeanne took a flash photo. Neither could ever make Mailer forget the other. What could Jeanne be doing now?

A Times Square bookie he barely knew was on the phone and a line queued behind him. Jeanne wouldn't speak with a din in the background anyway. She'd only say, "Ring me after the bombing, would you, dear?" He would get her from the street. Then, Podhoretz had to take a leak and—stout soul—he shook at the door in defiance of the lock. The drum-haired woman called out, "In a minute," and Adele, as an afterthought, hollered, "In ten minutes." Ten minutes? Ten pages were the initial litmus of a novel, able on or abandon. Ten minutes was the width of a woman's clock, her timetable of compatibility in bed or, in this case, in bed in the goddamned bathroom. In ten trembles of the clock, Adele would have a decisive answer as to whether or not Podhoretz would be allowed to urinate.

Where was the anger? It wasn't the liquor and the herb's fault since stupefaction never before drained his rage; on the contrary it always seemed to grant him permission. What, partial view observer status at his own public cuckolding? And to be unmanned by a woman? Was this not a blow to all mankind? He tried to work up a steam, but his head contained only gas. He moved to the door on the reflex intent of phoning Jeanne from the street. A woman in a tasseled dress handed him a copy of *Time* magazine with Khrushchev on the cover.

"Page forty-one, Norman. You'll be very interested."

That was all he needed, his name on the innuendo page or some critic dancing on the carcass of his reputation.

"What have I failed to do now?" he said.

———

The substratum on the stairway felt like a private party and he was surely not its host. Seated or standing, they all inched to the railings as he cut a stripe down the center and then someone said, "Out for air, Norm?" but translated into the vertiginous dialect of pot, drink, and cuckoldry, the voice was saying, "Out of air, Norm," and he half wondered if the guy didn't expect him to go someplace and fetch him a tall, cool drink of oxygen.

"Take your head out of your asshole," Norman said and listened for the laugh that didn't come.

George Plimpton, six feet and five inches of Ivy League erudition and pluck, gangly-cute as a baby llama, stood on the stoop, sharing a Cubano with a Negro too old and unprepossessing for his fedora and his blowfly shades. Plimpton was saying, "The definitive moniker was 'Mongoose.' You know, Mongoose Archie Moore? I've always enjoyed the inference that all of his opponents were venomous serpents."

Norman rolled the copy of *Time* and took aim just as Plimpton was taking a contented draw on the cigar. Sparks rained between him and the Negro. The Negro stepped back and hitched his trousers, maneuvering for room. Mailer said, "Stay out of this, Brother Ray," and tilted up until his eyes were level with Plimpton's conspicuously hollow gullet.

"Where's the think tank, pal?"

"The think—?"

"The School of Athens you were going to bring over here tonight."

"Norman, I phoned the fucking Algonquin and everyone is dead or in Los Angeles."

"Or both."

"Precisely," said Plimpton.

"What's on page forty-one?"

"What?"

"What's on page forty-one of this Pap smear?" Mailer said, dangling *Time*.

"How should I know?"

"Name me one literary scandal not bred in your hip pocket."

"Oh, for God's sake!"

"Let's see."

In the "People" section on page forty-one, he found Ernest Hemingway in the doorway of an emergency room, looking into the camera with his mouth open, his eyes huge. The blurb alongside the photo offered the news that he was undergoing voluntary electroshock treatments at the Mayo Clinic in Rochester. He was eating mostly oatmeal and onion soup, receiving very few visitors, and reading Stendahl's *The Red and the Black* and *Out of My League* by George Plimpton.

Norman said, "I thought you said you knew nothing about this?"

Plimpton glanced at the page.

"Oh, no. I heard it was only delirium tremens. Thank God, the man is reading at all."

"That's all you have to say?"

"Well, of course, I'm shocked and I'm . . . honored."

Mailer said, "Who's a venomous serpent, George?" and turned to quit Plimpton, but Plimpton said, "Norman, meet my barber John David Cronin."

He'd forgotten about the little man in the hepcat glasses.

"John David, will you tell Norman the slogan of your emporium?"

John David Cronin hitched his trousers a second time and rasped, "Clean your head; clear your mind."

---

There was a booth on Riverside, removed from the Broadway traffic and in the shade of a firefighter's memorial. Several times he'd used it to negotiate cessations of hostilities with Adele and it was the perfect spot to ring Lady Jeanne from. The booth was in sight and he would have gone ahead and entered it if he hadn't been distracted by the moonlight—he noticed it first in the phosphorescence of his wedding ring and wristwatch and in his shoeshine, and finally in the jewel bits of the asphalt. "Hello, Your Ladyship," he said, his eyes averted from the moon, his body English spelling "drift"—watch Brando, he never looks directly at a woman. "Pity you couldn't come to the party. I see you're dressed for it."

Instead of an answer he got more brilliance, which was what he wanted. He turned on his heel—the phone call would be redundant now. The moon made a lake of the wide front window of the park-side townhouse across the street, possibly tiered into three or four dwellings at this point; the window might belong to a private apartment or it might well be the seat of some esoteric foundation, Museum of Absolute Humidity, or some such drivel. The rich were so discreet and mad with their money. A potted fir grew without constriction against the glass and the green and off-green and moon-silvered needles forged a web of rhythm, a portrait of the logic of fire. Norman saw Jackson Pollock hovering in the air, hurling, spitting, and pissing at the window. He then repented with the aid of a long trowel, like a diamond thief with a pincer, until he realized that the very texture of his painting was laughing at him—flame being the ultimate giggle—and so he threw the trowel away and hurled and pissed, and spit once again. And the moon so loved the show that it stayed up for hours.

Silence. Norman and Pollock shared one common interest, the enhancement of silence. Pollock painted its portrait and Norman, in prose, could make it speak. Pollock learned the character of silence while tearing at a whiskey label—a paint scraper against a blackboard—while Norman thought he learned it first in the South Pacific. He could remember well the timbre of a soldier's furtive peeing against the tin bottom of a troop truck and the way in which the sound funneled ice up his spinal column.

*Ice?* Was that the name of that late Pollock he liked? Maybe a couple of years, maybe a couple of days before the joyride, raised enamel tapestry, the white acrylic piled, molded into furls, almost an icebound fountain spouting out of the canvas. Here silence really roared—one's entire head became encased in a seashell while looking at the painting. But a fountain? First, the fire and then the fountain? Did Jackson Pollock seek to play God backward?

Was the late painting called *White Ice?* No, he hung something even more B-movie on it, the same way he christened what passed for his juvenilia—*Moon Woman, Guardians of the Secret, The She-Wolf.* In Middle Pollock, you get only numbers, dates, and seasons. They say we all regress just before death. Once a man.

---

Up the hill on West End, some trouble boys gathered on the corner. They all had team jackets with HIVE stenciled on the back and they were yammering and floating in half circles with that no-place-to-pee intensity. One of them was giving another a haircut with a Barlow knife, sawing at the kid's back strands. Wait, no, he wasn't. Mailer had to stand still and squint. Each of them sported a medallion on a silver braid and the one kid was fixing the other's latch pin with the knife. The moon had gone behind a high-rise, so no telling in this light what sort of race they might have won.

"Nurse, I said, 'suture,'" Mailer said, coming close. The kids looked at him.

"The Five Hives, huh? Who's your rival gang? The Quintet of Dermatologists?"

One kid said, "Faggot flea market."

"What?"

"Where you got your Zorro shirt from."

"Look who's talking? Spades, wops, swishes, and women wear jewelry. What's your category?"

The kid with the Barlow turned to him and the other kid's medallion clattered on the ground.

"Aw, fuck," the kid said.

"El toro," the kid with the knife said.

"That's right, El Torso. Pleased to meet ya. You guys go to the Olympics?"

"We busted a window on Jew Street."

"I'm whole hebe. Watch your lip."

"Jews don't fight bulls," the one behind Norman said.

"Naw, they play the violin and figure out eternity, right? I'm running for mayor and your ignorance is the only thing gaining on me."

The kids laughed.

"Hey, I'm serious. Tell me, what'd you guys ever get from City Hall besides a curfew?"

The knife kid nodded out of the rope of his medallion and raised it high, catching a little of the refracted moon. Norman peered and read the words "Christophe Sanctus"; the medal was printed with the likeness of a white-bearded giant with a tribe of children on his shoulders. The kid tossed it to Norman. He eyed its glint as it was homing in on his forehead and he swatted it to the pavement, not trusting himself to catch it.

"Pick it up. You need it more 'n me," the kid said.

"Why? Where you think I'm traveling to?"

"To sleep."

The one behind Mailer pithed him with a boot heel and he was on his knees, feeling a rather pleasant nausea, an anticipatory hunger. The knife kid's boot was flying at his face and he tilted his head casually, as though to read the tread pattern. The laces whipped his temple and the kid was on his ass. The others were climbing Mailer's back. Serviceable jazz—Stan Kenton, maybe—was playing past a sleeper's window. Filtered through a corroded screen, the cadence of sleep, and the fugue of the night, it was as lonesome and clattering as a train going by and, like a train, it rendered the atmosphere prismatic; their punches were sequenced into stages and he could gauge the pain of each of the blows before they connected. He stood with two of them on his back. The knife kid rose and stepped in with his Barlow and Mailer swiveled for a pas de natural. The kid grafted to his right side inadvertently kicked the Barlow into the air.

Then they were running. Blood in his eyes and a train in his ears, the moon flashing now and again over the arch of a diminutive brownstone or through the gaps of the crossways, the kids' medallions flying in silver blurs about their necks, the fight forgotten, they were running to beat the wind up the street, and, defeated at each signpost, they simply renewed the race. Mailer remembered to breathe and his windpipe filled with acid. He slowed and the kids slowed. He brought it down to a trot and then a walk. They were in the middle of traffic with car horns sounding and sickly yellow headlights turning their skin to wax. The kids looked at him like (could it be?) they were expecting an apology.

"Hey, you guys want to come to a party? You could meet Tony Franciosa."

Smoke leaked from their mouths, yellow like their complexions. The gist of the respiratory conversation was "Aw, well." Walking away, Norman started to put his hand into his hip pocket. He felt something sharp against his leg. He looked down and saw that he had been holding the Barlow knife, open in his hand, since Ninety-seventh Street.

The party had swelled into the courtyard, the entire façade of the building burning like a jack-o'-lantern. Norman felt a seismic premonition in the pit of his stomach and longed only for an available toilet. The guests spotted him and quieted and then someone shouted, "Norman, you look like you've been in a war!" The only light in the basement was a bare bulb way in the back. He stepped over a tangle of loose cables, his sickness deepened by the association with serpents, smelling fiberglass now as well as wet rubber, mildew, and dog hair. The cauldron in his belly gurgled and a noxious bubble erupted in the base of his throat. A converted iron washtub hung on the wall, serving as the superintendent's sink, and, just above the rusting faucet nozzle and the equally rusting starfish-shaped hot and cold handles, the super had taped a full-faced close-up of Marilyn Monroe. Time and humidity had puckered the photo, her forehead and jaw were morphing forward with the artifice of caricature and this, combined with the powder tone of her skin, made Norman think of the evanescence of dreams. He redirected his attention to the hole in the sink and dredged the river in his gut—he brought up only spittle and a solitary bead of sweat from his forehead taunted him by piercing the dead center of the drain. He looked back up at Marilyn with watery eyes as he hung over the sink by axis of his thickening middle, inadvertently overexposing the photograph through the force of sheer longing. He watched helplessly as she faded to a white burn on the concrete wall. *White Light.* That was the name of that late Pollock painting. *White . . . Light.* We all regress before death. Twice a child.

---

Marilyn was in from the premiere of *The Misfits* and the wrap of her marriage to Arthur Miller. Encouraged by her East Coast doctor, she checked herself into the psyche ward of Columbia-Presbyterian. Well over a hundred correspondents and press photographers besieged the hospital and almost as many policemen were sent to the site, not to rout the army of the Fourth Estate, but merely to keep them quiet—there were sick people inside.

Every day another island of flowers passed through a succession of hands down a single unbroken corridor and into the incinerator out back—flowers did not match the décor of the ward—that is, until the press caught on. A petition made the rounds, trustees and benefactors were contacted, and a New York *Daily News* headline screamed, "*War of the Roses!*" Finally, a hospital spokesman announced that some of the flowers would be arrayed in the chapel and that Marilyn would be allowed to look at them, if she wished, for a half-hour each morning. When Norman heard about it, his irony monitor went off and he phoned friends to remind them that flowers were actually nothing other than the sex organs of plant life.

The crisis boosted her popularity beyond all reasonable expectation; this was indeed her finest hour, her greatest picture, albeit it was silent and it had no picture, but then again rumor was no new medium for her. At the end of twenty-three days, she appeared at the main entrance with a bouquet—a fresh one—in her arms and all of the honey taken out of her hair and replaced with platinum, saying only, "It was a nice rest," smiling and blowing kisses on her way to a limo, a blithe sleepwalker straight out of the Briar Rose legends.

Norman's photographer friend Costas wanted to get out of fashion and direct films, and Norman had gone hot on the same fantasy since he'd seen Robert Frank's celebrated rumpus with the Beat clan a few years back. It was something he could do when he couldn't write. He dialed Costas and cashed in nonexistent chips. Costas rented "original Ziegfeld costumes" from The Show Museum on Times Square and, through contacts, arranged a session with Marilyn in Susan Strasberg's flat on Sutton Place. Pumped with the mad adrenaline of wishful thinking, Mailer called *Esquire* and told them he surely could pull off an exclusive interview.

She was alone when Costas arrived, as somnolent as at her exit from the hospital, red-eyed as a jackal, and uninterested in the sherry he'd brought her. She floozied and flappered for the lens, charmed by the sequins and the beadwork, and talked of how famished for color she'd been in the hospital; she nearly fainted when they brought her down to the chapel of flowers and afterward she thought that the doctors had contrived a form of shock therapy for her, sans electrodes and written consent. Costas broached the subject of Norman Mailer and Marilyn said, "Talk to me about your friends who aren't famous."

"We'd be here all week."

"At least I wouldn't be here alone. You, me, and the rest of the run of the mills."

"You alone? I mean, look at all the people that love you."

"They're an eyesore," she said, curling her mouth.

"So, you know Mailer?" he tried again.

"Out in Hollywood, he's all they ever talk about."

"Really? The movie people? Why?"

"You read the papers?"

"Oh, jeez, that's all a lot of horseshit. He got drunk at a party and made a mistake. Anyway, he wants to interview you in the worst way."

"He wants inter-something in the worst way."

"Marilyn, it would be an *Esquire* cover. A chance to tell your own story in your own way."

She thought for a moment.

"If I want to tell my own story in my own way, what do I need a writer for?"

"C'mon, that makes no sense. What do you think you need?"

"I don't know. A friend?" she said.

Later she excused herself to take a bubble bath. Costas, as he told Norman, was there for four hours, from three P.M. to near to seven. The phone hadn't rung once.

---

Norman was astonished, he couldn't imagine not being liked by Marilyn Monroe, let alone having reason not to like her; goodwill was as much a part of her mystique as sex, and it was as though he'd just found out that God had something against him. He would have to eat cold crow for *Esquire* and doubtless the tale of her rebuff would become an instant legend (Costas was a friend, not a saint), a Hollywood and lit circle dinner ticket for years to come. He'd thought that the speed slalom of his marriage to Lady Jeanne Campbell-Mailer and his stay in Bellevue last year would be enough red meat to satisfy his detractors indefinitely. He could placate *Esquire* with a piece on her mystique and her relevance to the times, but he dreaded writing it, dreaded posting a valentine to Antarctica. Liz Taylor breezed into his mind in Marilyn's stead and just as quickly she evaporated. Night and day, thought Mailer.

There was a two P.M. showing of *The Misfits* at the Coronet and Mailer misjudged the midtown traffic and had to spend a twenty-minute eternity cursing the mottled plaster walls and the jazzy, lemon aisle lights of the theater. The non-history of the hour and the pseudo-history of the venue conjured the oblivion of afternoons in Bellevue and the few middle-aged women (but for the usher, he was the only man) who were taking this journey with him seemed all alike and all alone. One of them entered his row of seats just as the lights were dimming and sat two chairs across from him, blocking the aisle. She wore a fur and had a white prayer scarf tied around her head, and she nodded back and forth in her seat through the two trailers and opening moments of the film, as though the outing was for her only an exercise in thwarting insomnia. With Marilyn's entrance, she began to whisper in a hypnotized monotone. Tuning her in, Norman realized that she was reciting Marilyn's dialogue verbatim a full half-second before Marilyn herself. He would have been annoyed had it been a better film; the screenwriter was none other than Arthur Miller and he'd held to his penchant for romanticizing his characters to the point of vapidity. Miller hadn't understood Marilyn from go; upon marriage, he converted her to Reformed Judaism, which offered no prospect of heaven—Marilyn's very being asserted otherwise.

He couldn't help it; he moved a seat closer to the whisperer. The *Esquire* piece was coming together in his head. Marilyn-mania. GIs in bivouacs and clerks in rented rooms pinning up her photographs and lighting their lonely candles to her. Brain-dead East Side matrons reciting her movie dialogue like prayers. She was a Virgin Mary for our time. Her films, in which she never seemed to be playing anyone other than herself, were the equivalent of visitations. Between the lady's verbal mutterings and his mental ones, he lost track of the picture and was astonished when, during the achromatic stampede scene, the whisperer lurched over into the vacant seat that separated them and put her damp and electric hand in his, all the while prophesying dialogue that Norman guessed would be spoken a scene or two in the future. He did not know what to do and therefore he did nothing; the truth was that madness fascinated him and, in a strange sort of way, it intimidated him. In Bellevue he'd taken to scribbling the senseless monologues of wackos, hoping against hope for a silver lining of Joycean acumen. In sessions with his doctors afterward, he expressed regret that he wasn't going to measure up as much of a lunatic after all, whatever they, the outside world, and posterity might think to the contrary.

He worked up his nerve and turned his head to look at her. Even in the dark he could tell from her profile that she had been quite lovely once, but, like so many of her age and station, she was counteracting maturity with a façade of garishness—the dyed strands of her hair were more lustrous than the white of her scarf and the roseate oval on her cheek looked unlike anything but the bloom of some very rare pox. Norman hated this, hated the unwitting self-parody of the once beautiful and hated whatever urge it was that had them painting themselves as though they were their own undertakers. Without realizing exactly what he was doing, he reached over with his free hand and wiped at the blotch on her cheek. Much of the fevered stain came off in his fingers and he heard himself whisper, "No one's saying that you have to *act* your age." She turned in her seat and gave him the fullness of her face, his own fingerprints glimpsed dimly in the skewered tracing of rouge on her cheek. He saw who it was and realized—joy and terror—that he was having physical contact with her and she was not resisting.

In a tone neither raised nor lowered, Marilyn said, "In this business, you better not *look* it either." She reclaimed her hand as everyone in the theater turned to shush them, no one placing the voice they'd just been listening to for an hour and a half.

————

The last of the credits rolled away and the house lights came up. Marilyn already had her compact out. "Thanks a lot," she said, surveying the damage.

"I thought you were someone else."

She looked at him.

"Sorry."

"Well, you did see me through the picture. You're a pal for doing that."

"You were wonderful in the picture."

"You're a pal," she said again.

"You were."

"All right already. I'd rather go to a hanging."

Mailer wanted her to elaborate more than he wanted to protest.

"I did go to a hanging," she obliged him. "When they hang you with celluloid, it leaves no marks."

"So, why—?"

"Because I have to. My agent is signing me for a new one. Some farce with Dean Martin. I can't do a new one until I've seen the last one. How would I know who to be if I don't know who I am?"

She brought her compact up to her left eye, fitting it almost as though it were an outsized monocle. She bit at her lip.

"Know what Mr. Strasberg tells me?"

"What's that?"

"Spiders in your eyes, cobwebs in your brain," she answered, summoning up Lee Strasberg, lockjawed and cantankerous.

"My friend Costas tells me you don't sleep well."

"Why, did I sleep with him?"

"No, I meant—"

"I saw the contacts of his photographs of me the other day."

"And?"

"Don't ask me. You like to look at photographs of yourself?"

"Natives fear that the camera steals the soul."

"I've heard that. You know, seven, maybe eight years ago *Photoplay* had this promotion. The readers would choose what famous painter would do my portrait and then the magazine would hire the guy to really paint it. Some cranks or somethin' got together and sent in a majority vote for Jackson Pollock. That guy with the scribbles and splatters, right? *Photoplay* wouldn't have that so they made the runner-up the winner—some old Englishman with a white beard. Then this guy Jackson Pollock dies and I go with Arthur to see his show at that, that museum here in town where they have an outdoors? We come to this canvas, just caked, just bleached white and gleaming like a big third-degree burn on the wall. It's named *White Light*. Arthur, not knowing a thing because you never mention artists to artists, you know, says, 'Marilyn, that's you.'"

Norman needed a moment to answer.

"So," she said, "the camera's only a piece of hardware. It's souls that steal souls."

"I know Arthur from Brooklyn. Years ago."

"I guess I know him from the past, too. If I meet him in the future, then that'll be the past, you know what I mean?"

"No."

The lights began to dim.

"Could we talk some other place? I really don't want to see this thing again."

---

There was a place called Montanoso on First Avenue with black curtains and minute gold lettering on the glass. Marilyn entered with the self-possession of a regular and the maitre d' bowed to the floor to her and half the way to Mailer. Though the place was Andalusian, the décor was generic Roman ruins, timeworn bricks and a sheer muslin carpet stretched across the marble floor. At this pre-dinner hour it was totally empty and the maitre d' and the two waiters seemed to bristle with the alertness of house pets having bided the long day for their owner's return.

"Diego, the grotto," Marilyn said.

"Yes, Miss Mahn-roe."

They were led through the dining room to the edge of a curtained stairway. Marilyn stepped through the fabric and Norman politely waited for the maitre d' to pass through. The maitre d' smiled.

"No, the grotto I do not go."

The stairwell was winding, wooden and rickety and obviously not intended for the use of customers. He had in mind that Marilyn wanted to show him something and he didn't dare ask what it could be.

"What were we talking about?" she asked.

"Paintings, photographs."

"Yeah. I saw your picture in the paper once."

"Once?"

"The once I remember. You looked like the saddest man on earth."

"That would be the one where I was cuffed in the back of a wagon, right?"

"Yep. Must have been some party that night, right?"

"So what are you doing alone with me?" he asked.

"I might be just as alone without ya. What did your wife do to deserve it?"

"Nothing."

"So out of a clear, blue sky—"

"When's there ever a clear, blue sky? You're a method actress, aren't you? You gonna tell me that Strasberg never went into the logic of the events, the logic of the moment? You know when you're little and your mother tells you to go to bed? It could be . . . it could be your clear blue sky outside, high noon and the sun in every window. You do it. You go to bed. Something greater than you says to."

She didn't say anything so he added, "I'm sorry." In the air it sounded more dismissive than apologetic.

"So you hear voices?" she asked.

"Don't you?"

Marilyn said, "When I was in Columbia-Pres., they asked me

that question—again. I mean, shit, Marilyn Monroe, huzzahs and millions, so how come that question keeps coming up? Next, I'm going to hear a voice in my head asking me if I hear voices in my head."

They came to the bottom of the stairway and stood in a musty, tar-coated basement with pipe steam curling just over their heads. Marilyn took off her fur. On the floor there was an iron grate, cordoning off a subbasement, Norman thought. She reached down and yanked at the handle and the iron lock, secure in its slot, stood upright.

"Oh, you have the key," she said.

"No. What key?"

"Norman, you have the key in your pocket."

He put his hand in his pocket and took out a key, the kind he had not seen in thirty years, square-shaped with teeth on both edges. He handed it to her and she undid the lock and lifted the grate. Beneath it was a rectangle of coal-colored water, roiling like a stream. She twisted her arm up her back and undid the zipper of her dress. She put her hand to her throat and separated the garment from her skin. It made a rug around her ankle. She stepped out of it and wriggled her feet from her shoes. There were two or three women to Marilyn, Norman decided. This was her secret; a duo, or yes, even a trinity impacted, grafted onto the sweet essence of childhood itself. He had been right, she was the Virgin Mary—Mother, Daughter, Holy Ghost.

"Well," she said, snapping her bra off, the breasts popping free as though they were elasticized also, "didn't you want to go to bed?"

She stepped into the water without taking her eyes from his face. She was there and then she was not. He was standing and then he was on his knees, watching the torch of platinum fire falling away.

"Bed?"

<hr />

He had turned the faucet on somehow. He was warm and wet from his hairline down to his waist. The basement sink had no drainpipe and the water was also in his shoes. The Marilyn on the wall seemed thrilled that he'd returned to the world. He turned the tap off and shook his head and torso like a dog, the water every which way. He reached out and gave Marilyn a sloppy pat, the dark print of his hand staining her face.

The doorman slept at his post and the foyer and the stairs were purged by the hour, half-burned cigarettes, shredded napkins, and cocktail glasses here and there. He had never noticed before how the carpet on the stairs and the hallway absorbed the sound of one's footsteps, though he could feel the sloshing in his socks and read his progress in the footprints. Charmed by the discovery, Mailer tiptoed like a prowler through the opened door of his apartment. Adele and the woman with the bongo hair were lounging at either end of the sofa, both of them sipping gin, their mouths moving without dialogue. Enough was enough. He had to wake from these chain-linked dreams; he was going on *Nightbeat* in a few hours and he wasn't going to work in mime. He picked up the floor lamp and hurled it at the mirror above Adele's head. The lamp careened onto the sofa and partitioned the two of them. The impact brought the audio back and in the gossamer of the broken mirror he saw himself wearing an opera buffa crown. Adele looked at him with her hair highlighted by crystals. Neither she nor her friend wanted to be the first to laugh. He watched their lips curling into the pink of their gums. Adele opened her mouth but caught her laughter with a gasp, and for the first time he heard the *Toccata and Fugue,* low on the stereo.

"Adele, I want to go to bed," he said. The two women glanced at each other and then they reared back their heads and roared.

"He wants to go to bed," the woman got out. Mailer couldn't help smiling.

"Tell me, Norman . . ." Adele said, unable to finish, slipping back into hysterics. She leveled a finger at him and steadied herself to speak again. "Tell me, Norman," she said, "is that an amoeba in your pocket or are you just happy to see me?"

The other one lost her jaw; she let go a crow call.

Something in his pocket? He put his hand in to see what it could be. It was a hard object, metallic and cylindrical. He was fighting laughter himself now and the tears were welling. He had to hold it up to the light. Had he broken the light fixture as well? The light above was star-shaped and blinding.

"Bring gold, frankincense, and myrrh," he told Adele and Adele's girlfriend, not bothering to explain that he was alluding to another oddball light on high. "But mostly myrrh."

They stopped laughing.

Then he saw what it was in his hand. The trouble kid's Barlow knife.

**The Angel of Ubiquity**   The night nurse holds the paper thimble to the Duchess's mouth. The Duchess gulps the pills dry, not waiting for the water, because the acidic stripe that they paint upon the rim of her throat reminds her of the sensation of cigarettes.

"Drink, Duchess."

She sips the water. The nurse wipes at the film on her mouth with a tissue.

"What are you doing?"

"Shoveling the driveway, dear."

"I'd like my radio on."

"Well . . ."

"It reminds me that I'm alive."

"I thought that was my job."

The medication has melted into a pool in the hollow of her back. She feels the glimmering of the ripples as the nurse walks about—four worrisome steps to the door, a rotary movement back toward the bed.

"I'll leave it on low."

Even in dreams she doesn't forsake the presence of the nurse's station, the purr of the incoming calls and the muffled oratorios of their gauze-lined Remington Electrics. The station is nurse to her dreams, as is the radio. "*Kindertotenlieder*" plays hours before dawn. Breathing in tune with the melody, she is content to open her eyes. The angel of pestilence roosts at the end of her bed. The moon looks in through the window and the dark boughs of the angel's wings are warmer blankets still. She rises on her elbow.

"What brings you?"

"The wind. You will conceive."

———

"Nine . . . ten."

The nurse drops the clippers into the trench of her apron. Bits of the Duchess's armor scratch against the wall of the wastebasket.

"Do we feel lighter, Duchess?"

"Where am I?"

"You are right here with me in March the fourth, nineteen and eighty-one. We'll be going down to breakfast now."

The Duchess can walk but she doesn't like to until she has had her breakfast. The wheelchair trek to the cafeteria has the aspect of a morning carriage ride, a distant memory and maybe not even her own. So many of her lives were lived through borrowed eyes. Her favorite director, her beloved, and her least favorite lover, Mr. Hadrian, never spoke the words "film," "movies," or "pictures" in her presence. His medium was called "the projecting eye," as though the camera conjured everything. He would tell his actors, "In the projecting eye, you are all larger than you are." Often she has to repeat the maxim to herself when the clusters of memory make her feel not only a hundred years but also a hundred lifetimes old. This claim to grandiosity is also her answer to the curse of short-term senility, to the wintertide in her ankles and knees, to the romanticism of her failing eyesight, and to the reticence of her heartbeat. Now that she has lived all those lives, death seems, regardless, to be only one more predicted improbability, like the end of the universe or the coming of talking pictures.

---

Mr. Hadrian thought that his projecting eye outspoke language and outthought thought. He was a false Mediterranean, the son of a nuncio, he told his intimates. He palmed off his seminary Latin as a singular Roman dialect, and the furniture-dealing brothers who funded his movies and altered the world had no trouble believing him. They claimed to know cognates in the Yiddish of their mother and father, and both parties liked nothing better than to banter the yarning of imaginary linguistics into a cat's cradle, an entanglement of fellow feeling and enterprise. In much the same way they made millions together, albeit without any language at all—Hadrian had a feel for the Gothic and the furniture brothers were partial to horses and mahogany, and this placed them squarely in the neverland of the plantation with its equine marvels and elaborate interiors. Both parties smoked, both pressed cigars on near strangers, and this also carried over into the product since everyone in Hadrian's films, sometimes even the cloistered belles, puffed ambitiously. The early French cinematologists would pick up on this, writing that the time, place, and the populace of his movies seemed to be the chimeras of some rarefied inhalant. There were brooding squires in jodhpurs, leering minstrels in emblemized tailcoats, and the Duchess's prototypes, and eventually the Duchess herself, who outspoke language with the choreography of their eyes, often contradicting the testimony of the title cards.

Opting for the idyllic, Hadrian set his films in the era prior to the Civil War. He plotted them along precise biblical lines. Paradise was always regained when abolitionists sought to tamper with the established Babylon, when boll weevils deviled the crops and floodwaters hurled the levees, when industrialist Yankees trespassed south, bartering with gold that might as well have been alchemic since it had not, unlike the gentry's coinage, been gathered in the soil. At the end of these reels, there was hearth, home, and God, and there was the silence of adoration to underscore each.

Mr. Hadrian slept little. He passed the nights at the piano. His playing had an endearing quality of hesitancy, like a toddler's steps. There was the memory of a chord progression, which he heard, he said, drifting past a Venetian sporting house, the eyelets of the stone saints chipped from the cornice. He often said that if he could trap this memory beneath his fingertips, he was certain he would be serenaded with his first full night of sleep since adolescence.

Early in the evenings, an assistant would crawl up on the hide of the piano and flash glossies of possible bit players before Hadrian's eyes. He would look at the photos without expression, deferring the actual choices until the morning, when he would summon the exact cut of the faces he'd decided in favor of as though they appeared in a vivid dream. This is how he met the Duchess—he saw her that once without even interrupting the crawl of his hands along the ivories. At 8 A.M. he told his assistant, "I'd like the peach stones and the magpie wings at the front of the ball. Provide her with a corsage."

The assistant was inclined to think that Hadrian was referring to cheekbones and eyelashes. He had only to fan the deck of photos and to search through the garden of eaux de cologne at the far side—extra's end—of the commissary.

"Have you had your breakfast?" he asked, upon finding the Duchess.

She continued to stare into the imitator of *Photoplay* yawning on the tabletop, a publication called *Dreamazine,* her eyes huge in her coffee cup, saying nothing because she thought that the sufferance of his company might be the price of the meal.

"No matter," the assistant said, "some labors are better on an empty stomach. Let's get you into pictures."

She was outfitted in alternative trappings of lace and pinned with a corsage so fresh from the kill that it appeared to be weeping. The assistant guided her onto the greenhouse of the set and positioned her underneath a chandelier that swayed in counterpoint to the waltz the orchestra was playing (silence was so intricate then). The tallows dripped a circle of demarcation around her. Amid the bustle of the debutante ball, flame-handled swords and powdered bosoms whirling by, she dimmed her eyes in sync to the diminuendo of the waltz just as the camera's pan sought to reveal her; she knew, beyond articulation, that diffidence was a weapon and that mirage was the very soul of poetry.

Watching the rushes later, Hadrian held up his hand for darkness as her image swept across the screen. "Is there an animal that melts?" he asked his assistant.

However mystified, the assistant knew better than to ask Mr. Hadrian to backtrack on a direct question. "Well, a chameleon changes color," he answered, his finger tight on the projector's switch.

"But an animal that melts?"

"No. No, I wouldn't know what earthly good that sort of trait would serve."

"I see," said Hadrian. "Then it's a human quality I must have missed somehow."

Then later, when the picture had moved to another locale and the assistant was lulled into his private elsewhere as well, Hadrian said, "Do you know how we know the gods?"

"How?" said the assistant, his own knee-jerk response rousing him awake to the image of a wagon wheel detaching and taking on a separate orbit.

"In human qualities."

---

He began by buying her things. She allowed this, not wanting to seem ungrateful, but made no pretense of taking pleasure in the gifts. He studied her, perplexed that the presents brought no light to her eyes. He watched as she delighted in having her face painted in the predawn mirror and in the evening skin peel, which restored the porcelain of adolescence to her face. She had a native quality. She made icons of the technology beyond her scope of understanding. During the breaks in the filming, she remained on the set with her coffee stein, staring directly into the blind camera. Once, setting up a shot, he stole a look over his shoulder and caught her reaching out to touch the fishbowl lens. He let out a wail and she drew her hand back as though burnt.

She much preferred languor to luxuriance. Idleness was so sumptuous to her that she never wasted takes and she was loath to try the same scene twice. But she never tired. She reposed pert and wide-eyed in her canvas chair, waiting for the clapboard and the call of "Action." He kept telling her what hard work filmmaking was, only to reassure himself that he was living the same life he lived previous to meeting her. One day when the novelty dulled, she would wish she'd remained in the Burbank leather goods store that she prayed to be delivered from. He told her that for ten years, ten years of constant filming. He would say it to her in the screening room in the evenings, his droning so incongruous to the sweep of the zero-gravity dream on the wall that she could not help it, she would stand in the diamond tide of the projector and scream, "Silence!"

Desperate to figure her out, he abandoned what education he had and cross-referenced everything au courant, including Hopi underwater healing, which involved a pas de deux with one's reflected image on the surface of the swimming pool (this had something of a vogue in Hollywood of the early twenties since everyone in town over forty suffered the rheumatism and the gout of their good fortune), and the restorative powers of Eastern Indian time travel, which involved the use of antiquated maps and chanted charms—he kept reminding himself to mention at dinner parties that therapy of this sort could be seen as the overall justification of cinema.

One day he came to the simplification he'd been avoiding all the years he had known her. "Damn it," he told the Duchess, "it's that we live half our lives in dreams and if we don't dream we go mad."

"Isn't being mad a dream?" she answered.

He thought of angels. Throughout the Bible they were constantly delivering their messages with the Duchess's same barbed vacancy and then standing apart from the whirlwinds their epistles wrought, just as he'd watched the Duchess exit a burning barn, wrap herself in her shawl, and sit down to coffee without so much as a backward glance at the fire crew, their wagon, and their hoses. Over the course of six nights that were meant to be vacation time, doctor's orders, he worked out a full-length scenario of what he would later call *Low Country*. This was the story of the unfortunate messenger who sought the Madonna but was misdirected by a Galilean sandstorm into the stone garden at the front of a brothel. The angel came upon a young girl (the Duchess) naked beneath a muslin shift and clinging to a sapling shaped like a tau cross for fear that the storm would uproot it.

The angel knelt and took the shelter of the ibis, his wings shielding his head. The girl looked at the angel and mouthed through the howling sand, "What brings you?"

"The wind," the angel mouthed back.

Then, pitying the girl her beauty—obviously it was stigmatic of God's troublesome favor—he blurted out the message he was entrusted to give to the Madonna.

"You will conceive," he said.

With that, the sky cleared.

The angel thought it unwise to return to the kingdom and he was consoled to learn that the girl was indeed expecting. He nursed her through the pregnancy as crowds gathered in the stone garden and the tip of Orion's arrow dislodged from its moorings and came to rest directly above the house. On the evening of the miracle, he appeared in the foyer and asked the faithful to disperse and leave the household to its bereavement; the blessed one was born dead.

The angel remained under the awnings as the house burnt to its bone matrix and the false Madonna was dragged from her bed. The centerpiece of the garden was a pyramid of bleached pebbles. The crowd disassembled it within moments. However, the girl, through the error of heaven, was now an angel herself and the rocks passed through her like light and left her standing in a suit of halos. She took her nightgown off and spread it in the dirt. From the recent contact with her body, it glowed and gave off fine strands of smoke. She looked down at the dress and she said, "My child."

---

Urns of fruit were left for her at the outskirts of each city and town, more in mock-tribute than anything else. Angels, it was known, will drink from a well of silica but will not eat. At the touch of her hand, the fruit would calcify and become luminous. The townspeople gathered the moon rocks after she passed and then they would sweep her tracks from the dust. She passed through the ancient settlements and walked the desert until her cloak, borrowed from one of the stone-throwers on the night of the failed miracle, grew larval and her feet became thorny and webbed. Near the ravine at the edge of the ultima Thule, a demon appeared in the form of a shrub, stunted by climate into the form of a backward-leaning tau cross. The demon offered her her mortality back if she would disparage the Almighty. She parted her lips to reply and the earth swallowed her up.

She came to her senses, lying on her back in a garden of radiant fruit that opened onto a sporting house. The ground beneath her was charred from innumerable fires. The blackened grass blades nettled her spine like the very beard of the devil. She stood and ran into the house. There, drinking alone at the shelf along the window, was her angel of ruin. His wings had shriveled into two frayed draperies and an umbilical husk was visible through his tattered robes. She stood alongside him and he let her drink from his cup but refrained from looking at her until the Savior passed on the road outlying with his cross. The true Madonna followed and the averting of her holy eyes was the cruelest rebuke the girl-angel had ever known. She shed cold tears, deep in her abdomen, and she looked into the faded eyes of her companion. With great difficulty he uncurled his tongue from the base of his jaw. He said, "Do you . . . ?"—the rest of it rinsed cleanly from the Duchess's ear because the dream has hemorrhaged and her skull now wears the roaring bonnet of a broken pond.

"For the last time, Duchess, do you want to go for a walk?"

The magazine on the coffee table is open to a foldout of a pop cathedral in Montpellier. There are hanging crystalline features and a large, unmoored crucifix before the altar. The day nurse stands just beyond the phosphorescent steam—the airy ruins of the Duchess's sleep.

"Now or never."

---

She has drawn an intern. She likes them best for the gossamer of their hands. She must hold on as she walks, but this is through no particular lack of equilibrium. At each turn the fuse of her memory burns away. The journey is one of constant beginnings. A young hand is just the thing.

A woman, older than the Duchess, at least in appearance, sleeps on a gurney in a sea-green alcove. She is joined at the arm to a water tank, the liquid content of her dreams being deficient, poor thing. The projecting eye looks in on the ending. Mr. Hadrian dissolves to an infant's arm flailing at the rim of a Paleozoic bassinet. A title card flashes in her mind. Something about an ark of bulrushes and slime and pitch. Then, amid the nimbus of the therapy quarters, more old ones strain to genuflect before a length of pipe that extends across the entire room. She knows this scene well. The harvest holiday. Grandfolk preparing for the barn dance because to be alive at harvest is such ecstasy that they are quite willing to die for the privilege. The Duchess scores for organ as she passes.

"Did you know that music is the child of silence?" she asks the intern.

"Yes, ma'am. What's silence the child of?"

"God."

---

The old man who is much younger than the Duchess is waiting in the dayroom. He stands and opens his hands, anticipating a present. The Duchess looks at her own hands. She holds no gift.

"Mother Abigail," he says.

Now the Duchess places him. The old man who is younger is demented. He is the one who comes almost every Tuesday and she bears his madness for the sake of diversion—a queen and a queen's fool. At first she wasn't so sure since dementia and clairvoyance are such close cousins. Then one day he made the mistake of separating his lips (his smile is usually a grimace). She saw copper-stained teeth and the shell game of pure folly. She has nothing to fear from him.

The day nurse steers them to the sofa. Ghost heads float upon the surface of the room's black fish tank. No, rather, that is the dark glass of the coffee table and that is their own heads. His derangement has just the slightest quality of contagion. She leans forward, drawing up the battlements of her features, her eyes squinting like a snake's, daring him. He jerks his head closer also and his lips begin working without words, kissing air.

"I'm Hadrian Junior," he says.

Method, she thinks. He is balanced enough to have researched her past.

"It's just that the doctors say I have to keep reminding you."

"Of what?"

"Who I am."

"Which is?"

"Hadrian Junior. Hadrian Senior was your first husband. I'm actually your first son."

"How do you do?"

"Fine, thanks. You?"

"I had an operation."

"Devilment."

"What?"

"Did it . . . ? The operation, was it serious?"

She unsheathes her right foot from her furry house slipper.

"He made them thirty years younger."

"I see."

"It was the dark angel that did it. He brought me a message."

"Was it good news, mother?"

"I'm going to have a child."

The old man who is younger and mad starts to read the Mohammedan stitching along the rim of one of the sofa's throw pillows. There's a redness in his jowls and in the claw of his nose. He was sunburned in the ebullience of the same visitation that drove him cuckoo.

"So, I'm Hadrian Junior," he says again, finally.

"You told me."

"Oh, good. I mean, it's just that the doctors keep—"

"You told me."

"By goll, this is a good day. You're talkative, you're remembering."

"Do you have a message?"

"Pardon me, mother?"

"Do you have a message for me? Other than who you are and who my husband was, and who you think I am."

There's the pensive slosh of the saliva in his mouth and waves of befuddlement in the air between them, then the parting of his lips as his tongue misreads his mind's readiness to speak and the abomination of his teeth.

"There's a bit of a stir at the Temple. That's the Temple Mission Evangelical. My father Hadrian Covenant Lowry Senior began it and you expanded it after he passed away. You remember, mother, the radio ministry and later the Sunday morning television program?"

"Really?"

"Oh, yes. Aren't they giving you your fan mail? The Temple forwards it here to the home. It's like trying to redirect a blizzard. People remember, you can bet."

"What's the stir?"

"The stir? Oh, the stir. Yes, some of our congregation members have decided to boycott the collection plate and the charity appeals. You won't believe this, mother. They want to go to the movies?"

"What do they want to see?"

"Oh, it's not they want to see a particular picture. They want to be allowed, I mean, they want the Temple's blessing . . ."

"To go to the movies."

"Yes, good, mother. You know, my father Hadrian Senior, he held that still photography was on the square. A little rough on the corneas in his day, but square just the same. Moving pictures were another matter. All this manipulation of light and the human form by laymen and all of it in the service of thrill-seeking."

"Uh-huh."

"Of course, both light and the human form are significant reflections of the true nature, the eternal identity of God Almighty."

"Your father didn't like film?"

"He thought it would lead to devilment. From what I hear, he wasn't so awfully wrong."

She catches sight of his face in the mud surface of his coffee table. The opaque glass shrinks his jowls and smoothes the ravines beneath his eyes. He's waiting for the Duchess to respond and he is wearing the exact expression of a child trying to understand why he is being denied some looming euphoria beyond a marquee or deep in the belly of a circus tent. In one picture or another, she held this face to her bosom and spoke with her lips against the brow, telling it to age in order to understand.

"You ever get the urge to see a movie?" he asks, his voice now light and teasing.

"No, I prefer to live in the present."

"This has been such a good visit, mother."

---

Mr. Hadrian introduced the human presence to that pocket of the California desert and the crew—over two hundred of them—resented the journey and the long camp-over in Quonset huts. He carried with him a single trunk filled with the bank papers pertinent to the mortgaging of his villa and the Duchess's, as well as tarots and astrological charts, a spare suit, a Gnostic Bible, and the phone number of a Hollywood physician who specialized in nervous exhaustion that the furniture-dealing brothers had given him in lieu of funding. By the time he and the Duchess arrived, the preproduction crew had clapped together the hovels of an ancient boomtown. They painted pomegranates with glycerin in order to affect the girl-angel's glowing fruit garden.

The sparse footage that they shot remains now only in the Duchess's recollection. It blazed away long ago by virtue of its own nitrate content, and the Duchess's memory rates a close second in negligence. She remembers the sensation of the sky flaking away as the sand mills showered her with microscopic ore and she can vividly summon the opera house costume of the pituitary giant who played her angel. She also recalls Hadrian's annoyance with the tech wizards who could grant him no disruption of Orion, his own variant of the legend of the star of Bethlehem. This was how the trouble began. Livid one evening, he ordered all the cameras to be trained on the sky until dawn. Shooting did not resume with the day, nor with the next day. When asked what he was waiting for, Mr. Hadrian said, "A sign." The crew became impatient and wanted to know when they would begin again, and he looked at the sky and told them that they had "all the time in the world."

They stole away in pairs and fours. (Isn't there a symphony? the Duchess thinks. Haydn or Handel? The winds sneak off like thieves. Isn't there the counterpoint of their scraping chairs behind them and isn't the conductor left waving his wand at a sleeping tubist?) Certain that they would never be paid, they looted the film stock and properties, the dry provisions, carried off their desert igloos on their backs, and left Hadrian with only his bullhorn so that when his sign appeared he could command it in a sonorous voice. They drove off in their squat, armadillo-faced trucks, leaving the stripes of their desertion in the sand.

They had taken everything and there was a moderate wind that night. Mr. Hadrian and the Duchess woke in the morning, half-covered in a shifting blanket, to the cawing of a Packard's horn. They startled the eldest furniture merchant by disengaging themselves from the desert floor.

"Give you folks a lift?" he said.

The Duchess got in the car; she was out of clothes. She and the studio owner, whom she'd never previously seen anywhere near the front seat of a vehicle, drove off a few lengths. She cracked the car door and called to him. Hadrian stood there in a carpet of infinity. He drove and stopped. She called once more. The movie boss thought to cut his losses and she found herself half hanging from the hood like an ornamental roadkill. A white speck appeared on the horizon with a revolving party hat on and, sighting the boss's borrowed Packard, it sang out its two-note scale.

The boss said, "Do you see?" but she did not look at the ambulance and did not even open her eyes until the hills were in view. He asked, "Are you all right?" but all the time in the world was sieving away and its remnants lay stiff and heavy in the bowl of her jaw. She wished he would inquire about the time instead of her well-being. At least she would have known the answer.

———————————

She confesses the pregnancy to the night nurse, who promises to be helpful once the pains begin.

"Pains?" the Duchess says. "This is an occasion for joy."

"Really, Duchess, joy at your age."

"Well, when?"

"You decided on a name?"

"Abigail, if it has a sex."

The nurse starts to say something, but instead she only sours her mouth. She switches out the light and the aquatic vigil of the nurse's station seeps in through the doorway. Now and then bulky shadows take shape in the entryway and leap, for an instant, against the wall. She whispers, "Jump over the moon," the sound of her own voice making her realize that she is not asleep, though she'd assumed she was. She recognizes Schubert's *Unfinished* on the radio and she tries to recall her regrets.

She grows cross with her angel, having to wait.

How would you finish that? she thinks, as the symphony filters away and the announcer honors it with an epilogue of total silence. All this beginning, middle, and end business. That's the life of a caterpillar. Wasn't she a butterfly to begin with? The thrill of incompletion hits her. This was her secret all along. When she spoke with her eyes, she did so in half sentences, lending everything to interpretation.

---

In space, she thinks to herself, objects redirect light. That's Einstein, isn't it? He was the author of a new divinity, as grand and haphazard as all of the older ones. Hadrian, likewise.

Or is it light that redirects objects? It doesn't matter. It stands to reason; both parties would yield their paths. And get lost.

She and Hadrian, likewise.

---

God is lost. Filmed evidence of Him is moldering in forgotten vaults.

Where is her angel? He is a creature who carries darkness in plumes on his back and yet, tonight, he could not find his way in the dark. He has skulked into the east wing, a pediatric facility. He is teetering upon the bed board belonging to some newly tonsilless eight-year-old girl. She is asking him if she can bring her dog along.

He will realize his mistake when he feels the width of the child's finger against the hook of his fore-claw. He'll come before dawn. She will rise, in a vapor, out of the bed and he will say, "Do you see what I have spared you?" as she looks back at the husk of her body smoking on the bedsheet. She will answer, "Motherhood?" with a hitch in her voice because she is not so sure that their rendezvous isn't, in itself, a heavenly ordained form of procreation. Death is so fetal. Interim and mysteries. Waiting for the light.

Her angel will come soon, but he has never been this late before.

**The Name of the Dead**    Hey, Victor. Victor, c'mere, I want to ask you somethin'. I've known Tommy Roselli since I was twelve years old, right? So, what's the harm if I run back to the banquet room? I say, "Tommy, good to see ya. My prayers was with you all those years." In and out, Victor, what's the harm?

Mr. Magnasco says what? What do you even care what he says? Is he your Pope, your god, what? Listen to me, in two months' time Bobby Forlano gets to one of those spic cows that Magnasco fucks. He has her put a popper up the old bastard's nose that puts blood in more places than his underpants. Two months' time, Victor.

What do you mean? I was right about Stumpy Lombardozzi, wasn't I?

All right, then, Victor, have it your own way. Why should you listen to anything I say? I ain't nobody from nothin'. Crazy Cassandra, widow of the traitor, right? Go on and tell that to Bobby Forlano when he changes the sign outside and hands you a bus ticket out to Idaho. I'm tellin' ya there's gonna be some changes around here, maybe you oughta start payin' attention. You ain't standin' on no mountaintop, you know. Magnasco banks you on a bar, does that mean you got your story in *The Lives of the Saints* or somethin'? My Johnny Apollo he was a made guy, the genuine item. Even he couldn't take the changes. What's a hangnail like you gonna do?

Victor, Magnasco's goin' in the men's room. I could run back and say hello to Tommy. Vic, it'll take ten minutes for that old bladder to pump.

Hey, sure, I understand, you got your position to think about. What's it matter to you that I was back in that banquet room when you had a nine o'clock curfew?

Stay there. No, stay a minute; I want to show you somethin'. What's this, a throat lozenge for a hippopotamus? No, incorrect, this is the diamond ring of Johnny Apollo Salvatore Albergo and this is his neighborhood. This, in fact, is the same bar where Johnny Apollo once pulled four molars out of the mouth of a bookie who welshed Magnasco. This is where Johnny made his name and that's still a name that gets knees to knock all over white Brooklyn. Am I right, Victor?

I want you to do somethin' for me. Tonight, when you get off work, I want you to open the Bible and look in the Book of Ruth. Chapter four, verse ten, "Raise up the name of the dead upon his inheritance, that the name of the dead not be cut off from among his brethren."

You gonna apologize?

Accepted.

---

Hey, where you goin'? C'mon, would ya? It's over; it's piss under the bridge. Stay a second. I ever tell you how I met my Johnny

Apollo? What happened was my brother Hector got sent to the joint on a bum extortion rap. Wasn't no truth to it and his lawyers gated him in four months. But up in block nine, Attica State, he meets this bugs guinea who was so afraid of gettin' butt-raped that he asked the prison doctor to sew up his asshole.

The doctor hands him a needle and thread and says, "Knock yourself out."

Johnny says, "Doc, I'm in danger here. How you gonna help me?"

So, to get rid of him, more or less, the doctor gives him these super laxatives that they only prescribe to people who have terminal bowel cancer. The crazy, fuckin' wop didn't get off the toilet for two months and he was happy about it.

Now, my brother Hector, you know him?

No, you wouldn't. He's dead. Sweet guy, though. It was him that took pity on this fuckin' lunatic. He says to him, "This is my sister's number. Call her for comfort, ya nut wagon bastard."

You know, dial Cassandra for comfort.

So, anyway, one thing leads to the other and finally I take the bus up to Attica to meet this guy who's been callin' me every night. I'm sittin' there at the Plexiglas and they lead him in. I look at him and, uh . . . Okay, they don't expect you to wear stripes in the stir anymore, right? But this goomba strolls in in black Pierre Cardin casuals with leopard striped boots like he's getting' a guest shot on *Love Boat* or somethin'.

So, I says, "Johnny Apollo, huh? I thought you'd be a little taller, but all in all . . ."

And, Vic, he's sittin' there with this robot face on like maybe it takes a quarter to turn him on and make him talk, I swear.

I says, "Johnny, you okay?"

He says, "You gotta help me. They put something in my brain."

I says, "Just a minute here. What do you mean they put something in your brain?"

He says, "The warden had 'em stick a disk in there while I was under in the infirmary with the appendicitis. It works like remote control. I think what they want. I say what they want."

I tell him, "Okay, so what do you want me to do about it?"

He says, "Help me concentrate so I can block out their transmissions."

So, okay, I'll go along with that. He starts out, he goes, "My name is Johnny Apollo Salvatore Albergo."

I says, "Your name is Johnny Apollo Salvatore Albergo."

"I reside at 324 Mermaid Avenue."

"You reside at 324 Mermaid Avenue."

"You slut. I bet you got on ripped-crotch panties and you're moist as a fuckin' melon."

I says, "What the fuck?"

He says, "No, that wasn't me. They piped that in for me to say."

"C'mon, you crummy jailbird, tell the truth."

"No, really," he says. "They got me up all night sayin' the most horrible things to myself."

"Like what?" I says.

"They make me say, 'We are in control. We can take your freedom. We can take what you love. We can take your soul.'"

And, you know, just like anybody would after hearin' somethin' like that, I reached out my arms to him and he reached out his arms to me, and, right through that thick glass, I could feel him. Every atom of him. Right down to the heat of his blood, I could feel him.

---

No, c'mon, Victor, I'm fine. I don't need another shot. I've had enough.

A small one? Hell, why not? Just a splash. I don't know how you got me on the subject of glass walls. I mean, two people start out with a wall between them, where do they go from there? You wanna know somethin'? I swear every time I kissed him, I could taste hard, thick glass. Johnny Apollo had his own force field. He was a fuckin' alien, that guy. He knew it. He'd say, like, "C'mere, baby, lemme hold you." I'd lay my head on his chest and the heat of his body and the rush of his blood would be sayin', "You can't have me." You know, words you hear inside your head. "You can't have me. Don't even think about havin' me. I'm under glass for keeps. Go right ahead and worship me, but never think about havin' me."

---

Hey, Victor, who's that? Ya see? Over there by the buffet with the hat on and the fake fuzz around his chin. Is it?

Holy Christ, Carlo! Carlo! Hey, Carlo! Cassandra Albergo, hey!

Blow his cover? Blow his cover, my ass! He don't have to worry about a bust in here. He's got Italian Alzheimer's. Guineas never forget. He ain't a man.

I said, he ain't a man. He ain't even a man. Because, Victor, there are men and then there are MEN. A girl's lucky to have a man, sure—a guy that can give himself up, heart and soul. But you know what? In a way, she's luckier to have a MAN. A MAN cannot necessarily share himself with you emotionally, but, then again, he can be observed and learned from.

You know?

Life's got a lot of lessons to it, maybe you and me didn't learn the same ones. But, Johnny . . . Well, it was like Johnny chose me to be the one who knew him best. He chose me to be the one who really knew what he was worth.

So, you knew my Johnny Apollo, right?

What'd you think of him?

Well, where the fuck was you when we was carvin' his tombstone? Wallpaper is "all right." My Johnny Apollo deserves to be spoken of with just a little bit more respect than that.

No, no, listen. Listen to me. Johnny Apollo was big enough to take swipes from guys like you. That ain't what bothers me. It's just that the years go by and you guys stay stuck in your little worlds. You wouldn't know the truth from a bag of bricks. Johnny was a free man, you understand? You're a free man; you cannot be chained to somebody's idea of how you should act. Right? But Johnny—I mean the position he was in—he had to inspire faith, had to have people believin' in him. Huh? It's a fine line Johnny had to walk and he walked it. He was his own; he had his own.

I tell ya . . . Wait, hold on. There was this one night when Johnny came in late with the boys. I get up and I figure I'll fix an early breakfast. Johnny comes in the kitchen. He says, nope, nobody's hungry. He's got this big shopping bag in his hand. I says, "Johnny, what's in the bag?"

Johnny says, "We're goin' into the lingerie business. John Public can stuff his ol' lady into this garbage. We'll make out like bandits."

"Oh, yeah?"

I know. Oh, I know, Johnny. It was just the feel of those whore things in my hands. It was the whiskey on your breath and the way your eyes wouldn't stay still. I knew what you were going to say next.

You said, "We gotta check this stuff out. The boys are trustin' me with their money and, hell, I'm trustin' them with my life. There's a lot of guys out there with good reasons to kill me. My boys are all that stand between me and the bullets. That's the same place you're standin', isn't it?"

And I know. Even before everything, I know. Johnny's gonna hold my hand. He's gonna stroke my hair. He's gonna kiss my face with Carlo over there on top of me. He's gonna whisper in my ear, "Are you thinkin' about me, Cass?"

Yes. Yes, Johnny. I was thinking about you. Why are you smiling? Why are you smiling that hungry smile? Look. Right there. There's blood on your shirt. Jesus, there's blood in your smile. Now, you're on your knees. You have to stop. Please, you have to stop. Johnny, please, you have to stop right now.

Johnny!

---

Vic, what the fuck happened here? I got whiskey down my tits.

Passed out? Get off it, I was catnappin', sure as anything. Whyn't you set me up again?

No, I didn't say I want somebody to walk me home. I said, set me up.

Please.

What do you mean no?

You mean, like, no, you are denying the widow of Johnny Apollo a drink? You're riskin' a bolt of lightning and a clap of thunder there, Victor. After what I've been through, God in heaven would serve me stupid.

Much obliged.

Hey, where you goin'? Hold it, I wanna ask you somethin'. You think they got liquor in heaven? Supposed to be paradise, right? You know my Johnny Apollo—twelve years of marriage—he could not get to sleep without a drink. You wanna know somethin' I never told nobody? Right after he died, I couldn't sleep for worryin' about him. I'd sneak down to the cemetery after midnight and I'd pour Johnny Red on Johnny's grave. True story.

He used to tell everybody that I could predict the future. You remember that? Well, I still can. Don't too many people come to ask me for the lowdown anymore, though. What do you say you and me have a little look in the crystal ball right now, all right?

What, are you scared?

Two months' time, Victor. Sixty short days. Mr. Magnasco's in the churchyard and Bobby Forlano's all over this place like rot on rot. Crème de la cocaine on the cash and carry across the bar. Magdalena, Sylvia, and Mercedes, and some iniquity in the rooms upstairs. You're gonna make more than you ever dreamed if you're smart enough to get up tomorrow morning and go make friends with Forlano.

Yeah, right, you'd hop in Magnasco's grave right after him. C'mon, I know how it is with you; loyalty don't load your stomach. Besides, you gotta provide for your declining years. You got things to look forward to, you know? Like rheumatism, arthritis, and a fuckin' plastic lung. Like your little grandkids jammin' sticks in the spokes of your wheelchair. Take what you can get, Vic. That's the kinda guy you are. Now, you take my Johnny Apollo . . .

Wait, what do you mean you take Johnny Apollo? You can't take him. Nobody takes him. I couldn't take him and I couldn't have him. He couldn't breed, he couldn't love, he couldn't be loved, he couldn't grow old. I mean, what a beautiful, fuckin' spaceman that guy was.

---

Hey! Hey, Victor, where'd you go? Hey, where is everybody? What, did I say somethin' to spoil the party? Jesus Christmas, I'm sorry. You know what I'm gonna do to square things? I'm gonna squat down and take a piss right where I'm standin'. And you know what else? While I'm doin' it, I'm gonna quote from the Bible.

Now, hear this: "Raise up the name of the dead upon his inheritance, that the name of the dead not be cut off from among his brethren!" Words to live by! If you're already dead!

Oh, Jesus, no. Kelly Christ, I didn't know anybody was there. What a fuckin' fool I'm makin' of myself. Look, I'm sorry. Come on out where I can see ya and I'll give ya a proper apology. What are you drinkin'?

Johnny? Holy Mother of God, Johnny Apollo! There's a rumor goin' around that you're dead! Don't fuckin' tell me! Don't fuckin' tell me, Johnny!

Hey, where did you get that suit?

Well, it's too tight in the shoulders and it crawls right up your ass. You look like a guy tryin' to be a faggot for the first time.

Aw, forget it. Leave the suit. Maybe it'll grow on one of us. So, what's up with you?

Peace talks? Seems like we been through this before, John. Magnasco, Forlano, it never ends with those guys. I tell you what, you stay here with me tonight and you let Carlo and the boys and ol' man Magnasco . . .

No, no way. No way under God.

Johnny, you didn't hear me. I said, no. I'm definitely not goin' out tonight, and double definitely not to no Arab joint. I have to go to the bathroom just thinkin' about that kinda food.

Whoa, slow down a minute.

Hey, would you listen?

What?

Oh, is that so? Well, in that case, fuck you. Fuck you, fuck you, fuck you.

Don't!

---

Got a cigarette?

I said, you got a cigarette?

Maybe a light to go with that?

Thanks. You know, this is strange. Look around you, Johnny, this is very strange. A luncheonette, a diner—the sorta places people usually go to settle their differences—that wouldn't do for you guys. You gotta have lava lamps and bitches with sapphires in their stomachs.

You hear that?

I said, did you hear that? Tomb-takada-tomb-takada-tomb. Sounds like somebody beatin' a kettle in hell. Why don't you guys just go kiss and make up in Beirut, for Chrissake?

Where'd you go? That fuckin' man of mine, I can't turn my back one second.

Excuse me, could I get through?

Pardon me, I wonder if I could pass.

Move it!

Ow!

Excuse me, Omar. Yes, you with the roll of Charmin on your head. I need my left tit to keep my husband happy, if you don't mind too much. You elbow me again, your own camel won't even recognize you.

Carlo! Yo, Carlo, I'm talkin' to you! You seen my husband?

In the back? Is Magnasco with him?

Is Bobby Forlano there?

Carlo, I'm talkin' to you!

Johnny, there you are. You left me alone out here. So, what happened? You guys make peace?

No peace, what does that mean?

Slow down, okay?

Okay, but what?

No peace, but you accepted your punishment? For what?

All right, what you're sayin' to me, Johnny, is that you set up Mr. Magnasco with Bobby Forlano and, to cool this thing out for keeps, Forlano's given you up as a rat. That is what you are sayin' to me, right?

Okay. Okay, now, why would you do a thing like that? I mean, Magnasco's like your father.

You wanted your inheritance early.

You know, I think maybe I might be takin' in a little too much information a little too rapidly. What I need to know is just one thing. Johnny, what is this punishment you are talking about?

They want to kill you in front of your wife?

———————

Where's the fuckin' camera? Can you believe you had me goin'? How long have you guys been plannin' this stunt?

Guys, you got me about to bust a gut, already. Enough's enough.

You want me to play along? You want me to play along? Okay, Mr. Magnasco, Mr. Forlano, Carlo, wherever the fuck you went to, Johnny, I just wanna say thank you for a lovely evening. I'd like to stay longer, but I just had this dress dry-cleaned. I don't want any of that Kool-Aid my husband calls his blood on it.

Who'll take a lady home?

———————

Johnny!

Oh, God, Johnny, lay still. Ya see, I got it? I'm holdin' it. I'm not gonna let you go like this. God, no. Call an ambulance, you fuckin' bastards.

Johnny, can you hear me? I want you to tell me you love me. Just say it. Please.

Okay, if you can't talk, then blink. Blink your eyes one time if you love me. Just do it, once.

Oh, no.

———————

And so heaven says, "Raise up the name of the dead upon his inheritance, that the name of the dead not be cut off from among his brethren."

But my Johnny got his name from his father, his death from his brothers, and his inheritance from no one but himself. What's there left for me to give him?

But up?

And where do you go to get a divorce from a dead man?

Here. This is the place you go and this is the place you stay.

So, Victor, where are ya? Set a lady up. It's a long time 'til morning.

**Schism**    In 1378, the Cardinal College, comprised of a majority of Frenchmen, declared the papacy of Urban VI, an Italian, void and named Robert of Geneva as their new Pope. He would take the name Clement VII and reside in Avignon. Urban VI remained in office in Rome and both contestants to the holiest of offices excommunicated the other and their followers.

Catherine of Siena was visiting Rome at the time. When she heard the news she retired to her lodgings, lay back on her wooden pallet, and called for her scribe. She ordered that the letter she was going to dictate be delivered to both Popes, numerous members of the higher clergy, and Christian heads of state, as well as to the Grand Turk, whom she dropped a line to now and again in hopes of redeeming his immortal soul. Although he was her hated enemy, she would not dream of issuing a major proclamation behind his heathen back. Catherine said that though she reserved for herself the title of Messenger of God, the holder of the papacy represented no less than the Almighty's shadow upon the earth. The fact that there were now two shadows alighting on separate and warring countries was too much for her to bear; her body was vivisected, her heart was carved in twain, and she proposed to die at her earliest convenience.

The letters were dispatched and no one believed her. Since girlhood she had survived solely on the communion tablet and a few spoonfuls of vegetable broth a day; she weathered a certain variety of pox that returned strapping young men to God in their sleep, and in times of plague she mothered the infected unto the hour of their deaths. Urban VI, whom she nominally supported in her letter and who had been trying to get her to return to Siena and leave him in the comparative tranquility of a mere papal schism and untold assassins vying for the honor of doing him in, offered to have her transported via map sheath to the top of the Alps so that she could roll over into the arms of God at her pleasure. The Grand Turk—prey to the fiction of Catherine's beauty—replied that she should come and die in his gold-spun hammock. Clement VII had been acquainted with her in Italy years before and he'd never gotten over the tunic of goat's hair she received her visitors in. He inquired if any part of her wardrobe might be made available following her demise.

Catherine lay on the pallet for just under two years, taking neither food nor water, sucking her finger, tweaking her ear, and praying to die. Her scribe brought a truncheon into the room one day and she told him to hold his horses, whereupon he tied a rope around the nearest tree and hung himself. An anonymous priest—so many of them came to gawk that Catherine stopped bothering to ask their names and affiliations—took it upon himself to come and shrive her, and she humored him by saying that she vaguely envied the Virgin her immaculacy, possibly meaning that she could have done without those darned menstrual cycles.

She couldn't think of anything else. Brother Marcantonio of Spoleto, a convivial Franciscan very loosely attached to the monastery of Saint Ambrose and known to us only because he wrote a self-serving memoir, came with victuals, just in case, and would sometimes read to her from his *Book of Odes*. She politely asked that he postpone the recitations until after her funeral. Guglielmo of Rovigo, an expelled Carthusian, arrived with the flush of the dawn for six straight weeks in March and April of 1379 and flagellated himself just outside her doors, deaf to her entreaties for him to go away. He severely injured his spinal column in the course of the beatings and was later able to pass himself off as a victim of lightning; he found employment with a traveling carnival, posing as various members of the alphabet. He is pictured in a famous series of woodcuts by Zuccinno, contorting his person into the constituent letters of the Italian word *pazzo*.

The withholding of death, despite her efforts, was the last desperate ploy of Satan, and Catherine told herself that she must be patient and tranquil. She mused on the five wounds of the Crucifixion, emptying her mind of all other thoughts. Her surroundings and even her own person began to recede into an ashen impasto while the florid wounds bloomed in the air, a quincuncial optical stigmata. The remaining visitors arrived to find her pallet empty and the cloistered air of the room pungent with blood. They pestered Urban with news of a forced assumption. God, they surmised, was the one who had abducted her and in the end He had been forced to kill her to get her to go with Him. Urban was busy purging his new Cardinal College, only a few months old, and buying up the services of mercenaries with indulgences that all but guaranteed heaven and would make life hell for the rest of Rome for years to come. He proposed that perhaps Catherine went to the market to get something for dinner and he asked not to be troubled with the matter again unless she turned up alive and was willing to take up arms in defense of the Papal States—every hand was needed. In her limbo between the worlds, Catherine gave up on prayer and wrote one unending mental letter to herself, and the crowds—gathered outside her lodgings in hopes of a visitation or at least a glimpse of a honey-colored ray of light—heard a softly whispered patter, as though a single mouse were scurrying across the shelf of their collective mind.

The dying Catherine pitied the one who had lived her illiteracy. She'd heard the Word of course; she was sermonized from the hour of her birth. She breathed in the Gehenna of the Dominicans, Franciscans, Benedictines, Waldenses, and heretics under no particular banner save that of lunacy, but Urban's predecessor Gregory XI made a point of showing her his Papal Library, or, as he called it, his "nursery of the mind." The ordered scrolls and folios, with their colored ribbons and leaden seals, indeed held all the grandiosity and all the mystery of flowers. Gregory allowed her to open a few of the illuminated parchments and she found rows and rows of charmed candle flames, the calligraphy as mellifluous to her eye as the sound of this same Latin—a separate enigma to her—was to her ear. Ever after, she scrutinized her own dictated letters for evidence of her own personality. She was reassured by the visual harmony of the alphabet, but she ached to connect sight with sound as she yearned for some sensory perception of her God, yes, other than His wounds, which seemed too human to be trusted. Couldn't she just once hear His voice? No? Well, perhaps He would see fit to write her a letter? What colors would He write in?

Wait. Hold on a minute. Words gave solid form to . . . Oh, yes, in the beginning was the Word and the Word was with God, and the Word was God, unspoken, unwritten, even unknowable outside of the Void that was with God and the Void that was God. Why did the living Catherine never see the danger—the looming threat of iconolatry that these pretty painted Words brought? Could she have been that ignorant? Of course, she was ignorant. Wasn't ignorance a part of faith, a willful denial not unlike the denials of the flesh that emaciated her body and sustained her soul? Ignorance gave solid form to the soul, a voice in pitch silence, an entity in the Void, something in the dark. Knowledge was something separate from intelligence. The intelligent were forced to ask questions; the ignorant only knew. But given all that, wasn't the Word still the Word if it was seen instead of heard? Wait, whose Words were they, anyway? Which hand guided the scribe's hand? In the scriptoriums of the Turk, they wrote with liquid gold upon marbleized paper. No? And if this corporeal body of the Word was to be trusted, why was it that it had to be taught? You were taught to read and to write, but you heard and you spoke . . . on faith?

"You told me what to say in those letters," Catherine said, trying to rise from her pallet and proving conclusively to herself that she no longer possessed a body. "I confess I threw in a phrase of my own here and there to make them seem . . . well, lifelike, I guess. Do You think You can speak like me? What do You know about me anyway?"

She forced herself to recall the sensation of rising after a long sleep, the waterfall of the bodily fluids, the creamy foam lathering in her head. A wind stirred in the room. The five wounds of Christ Crucified began to bleed.

"Don't. Don't try that now. If You can cry, You can speak. Stands to reason, even for a mystery, right? No, You can't speak, can You? If You could, You'd command me to be silent? Cat got Your . . . ? Oh, You poor jaded fool. You envied me my voice. Isn't that it? Well, take it, I curse it. Just leave me scales to sing in my own head. You know, scales? Ascending scales? Imagine if You hadn't thought of words. G major, the entirety of the Book of Matthew, G minor, the Gospel According to Saint Mark. So forth. After all, it's how You think, isn't it? In song? They always said that it was. So, think about it. Oh, this is useless. What do You have to do with music? I wouldn't put it past You to think in graphs and clocks. You know time, sure; eternity, I mean. That's the one gift You kept for yourself and so we invented music with a beginning, a middle, and an open end. If we were undying like You, there would be no music, would there? Do You know something, Sire? I'm blind to the mystery of eternity, I may not have known how to live, and it's obvious that I don't know how to die, but You, Sire, are miserably tone deaf."

If she had eyes, she would have closed them. Instead, she willed herself to go blind. She died then and there of unhappiness. On the pretext of showering her bed with rose petals, which was a vanity she never would have abided, Brother Marcantonio of Spoleto entered the room early in the morning, only to see her temporal remains restored on the pallet. The odor of sanctity was present, but it turned out not to be the aroma of wood-cut violets that everyone expected. According to Marcantonio, it was something entirely more forthright, a bit like the boot-blackening smell of the shoemaker's stalls or the unique fragrance of a rubricator's dipping well. Cardinal Uzzo solicited for the return of her body to Siena, and Urban offered to provide the wheelbarrow, but the Collegium begged to take charge of the affair. There had been martyrs among the new College, but no new saints, which is what Rome desperately needed now. Siena was told that the absence of putrefaction had to be established if the process of sainthood was to go forward and Catherine was taken to the Chiesadi Santa Maria Sopra Minerva, and remained on indefinite loan there. In the meantime, Siena appropriated the house she had grown up in on Via di Sant' Antonio, converted some of the rooms into chapels, commissioned frescos by Sodoma and others, and called it the "Santuario Cateriniano." When Rome saw fit to make them a present of her head in the fifteenth century, Siena housed it in the tabernacle of the church of Santo Domenico. They dressed the head, the story goes, in a length of material from the Sabbath dress of the adolescent Madonna.

---

In 1974, Father Bernardo Rizzolo, Ph.D., was appointed prefect of Santo Domenico. He wanted nothing to do with the actual pastorship; daily mass was a six A.M. formality allotted to the ancient Father Burgio, who as late as 1980 continued to single out Rossellini for vituperation and to offer up the odd prayer for the continued good health of the Duce. Rizzolo's tasks were to write press releases, see to the conservation of the artwork done by the studios of the fortunate Renaissance dabblers endowed with enough money to bribe the archdiocese, and to diplomatically reject the petitions of scholars, scientists, and even paleoanthropologists who wanted to see Catherine's head. Strangely, or perhaps not so strangely, these suits were all brought by foreigners. Rizzolo gave it little thought; in Italy, after all, everyone feared the *occhio maligno*. He was fearful himself and he had one quarter of a mind to curse his fate and the ever-nearing hour when he would hold that head between his two hands and look into those floating Caravaggesque eyes. Oh, the peril of those answered prayers.

Rizzolo took holy orders at seventeen. Almost a decade earlier he had given himself in betrothal to one of Sodoma's reflections of her in the Santuario Cateriniano. He told the news to his father, an engineer who had grown up under the nerve-strain of Catherine's omnipresence and even sometimes joked of constructing an incorporeal bomb powerful enough to rid Siena of her for good. The son was told to go to the dictionary and look up the word "necromancer." Undoubtedly, the father meant to use the word "necrophile" and, who knows, that definition might have dissuaded the boy. The entry for "necromancer" spoke of a "sorcerer" who communicated with the dead and divined the future. Like a priest?

In his doctoral dissertation written at the seminary in Rome when he was all of twenty-one, Rizzolo sought out not the actual saint, but the Catherine of pseudohistory, lore, and literary wish fulfillment through the ages. This was she who plucked up a severed eye after some fictitious battle with invaders on the Piazza de Campo and held it trembling in her hand until it stilled and pointed north. She walked all the way to Bologna, where she found the vanquished and one-eyed foreign mercenary begging alms, with a fake accent, at the city's gates. This was the Catherine who, in a pinch, would scrawl a message onto the belly of a pigeon and shoo the bird off to find His Holiness or the Holy Roman Emperor. The bird would return only to roost in her palm and unfurl its plumes so that she could read the reply. This was the Saint Catherine of the people. Rizzolo made much of the fact that some holy vessels—George, Philomena, Christopher—progressed from fiction to sainthood, but was it not true that Catherine of Siena made the opposite journey? And was this not an inspired form of ubiquity?

---

On the first evening of his curatorship, Rizzolo groomed his hair with brilliantine and wore a paisley neckerchief over his collar. He brought pillows to the chapel, bolted the door, and made a divan of the front pew. There were all sorts of possible opening ploys. For instance, he could bring in a stereo system and play period music softly. He could write a haiku of love upon the emerald leather of a dried ivy leaf, sign it with a Latinization of his name, and slip it through the vent of the tabernacle. He gloried in these ideas, but knew in his heart that they were out of the question. Even in her letters to the Pope, Catherine pretended to speak as an ordinary woman and this forced upon Rizzolo the conceit of his lifetime, the role of the ordinary man. Suppose they met in a stunted elevator or in the turret of the hastily locked belfry in some ancient church. Their conversation would be at first tentative, deferential and solicitous and, little by little, they would thaw the distances between them by mentioning common acquaintances and drawing out common interests.

After introducing himself as "Prefect Dr. Bernardus Rizzolo" and touching upon his dissertation, which was on the shelf of every ecumenical library of standing in Christendom, he looked off, faked a yawn, fluttering his hand at his mouth like a trumpeter with a mute, and said, "You know I have a good friend in Florence who owns a reputable osteria. His name is Paulo Gianono. Did you know the Bishop Pierantonio Gianono? You know, the fellow who refused a red hat from Urban for piety's sake? He woke up the next morning and his courtyard was full of conical yellow hats. Did you know that he's my friend Paulo's uncle, if you discount the fourteen or fifteen generations between them? What's time, anyway? It's dull and self-serving to think of time as loss and decay, don't you think? On the other hand, when people try to put time in a positive light, they speak of progress and evolution. That's really all so abstract and peripheral. Day to day, year to year, what is time? It's an Easter hunt for the bright egg of identity and the hunt is always in unfamiliar fields, if you will. If you'll forgive me, I had a dream once that truly defined the concept for me. I was on a surgeon's table and it was some strange, high-pressure situation where you had to tell the doctor exactly what you wanted taken out. There was a long line of gurneys behind and invalids jabbering for me to make up my mind. The surgeon, fish blade in hand, asked his question and I said, 'Take out my inner child.' Not because I wanted him eradicated, but because I wanted to have a conversation with him. Face to face."

He listened for a possible wind through the rafters.

"I suppose people would think this is ludicrous, you and I talking like this. Some sort of delayed funeral rite, I guess they'd think. I really couldn't feel less like that. I'm inclined to see this as more of a baptism. I can't help but feel that I'm bringing a fragile, squirming soul back into the light of the world. Oh, not that you've ever really been away, but the ecstasy of belief is a thing for the moment. Our entire faith is contingent upon reaffirmation after reaffirmation, isn't it? Rebirth after rebirth, even."

Still no rustling above.

"I think I'll let you sleep now, signora. I call you signora because I consider you wed to our Savior Jesus Christ. I promise I will extend the very same courtesy and devotion to you that I would to my dear friend's wife."

He got up and lit every tallow in the prayer well. He pressed ten thousand lire into the poor box and returned to the pew. He closed his eyes and pretended to go to sleep.

---

Over time he sneaked in an entire hi-fi, hiding it in an anteroom, wiring and unwiring it at the waxing and waning of the night watch. He played Mozart's *Requiem Mass in D* for her while conducting an invisible choir, spasmodically shaping the notes in the air amid the haze of burning sandalwood.

"A Freemason, of all things, signora," he said in an aside and then stretched the arc of the soprano's lingering B-flat in the air as though showing a length of yarn to a spacecraft. "An evil man repenting with the last breaths of his mortal body. They're always the best instruments, aren't they?"

He brought in a period chess set, removed the bracket of candles from the prayer stand, and set the board up on the steps of the sacristy. He taught her the fundamentals painstakingly— she'd had no time to learn the game in life. He anticipated her aptitude for it; it was a contest based upon rhetoric, argument, and will, after all, and he saw fit to allow her a sly forbearance in the early stages of the matches and a gentle and firm blitz- krieg later on. His pawns were untouched, his knights were be- guiled into surrender, his bishops were overridden, his queen circumvented, and his king possessed. Time and again, he was left to contemplate the checkered emptiness of his side of the game board.

---

It was All Souls' Eve and a lunar eclipse was scheduled for the early morning hours. Such heavenly ordained irony was not to be ignored, not to be wasted. Rizzolo apologized for leaving the chess set at home and he begged to be allowed to speak freely. It was time for a heart-to-heart, never mind the obvious about hers residing, technically, in Rome. There were one or two things the signora did not know about him. For instance, entering the priesthood hadn't been his idea any more than this evening's dis- ruption of the heavens was the product of any earthly referen- dum. He, like the earth, was a victim of gravitational slavery and, worse, there'd always been a confounding obstruction between him and the exalted face of our Lord.

"This obstruction I speak of . . . Forgive me, I really must re- phrase that. To be precise, it is not an obstruction. It's a self- ordained stigmata of the eye, an hysterical blindness of my soul. Signora, I look to find the Lord, but I see only your face and all the rest is darkness and darkness's aurora. At the northernmost part of our night tonight, the earth will go blind. Signora, I would touch you and look at you. I know you will object, but did you never lay on hands? Did you never embrace the condemned, lie with the dying, carry the crippled? Did you not? I remind you, signora. August, thirteen seventy-nine. Alfonso Il Magnamino, the warrior of Padua, writes to you about the danger of dying of the sin of pride. 'Sister, I implore you. I have looked into the face of death and have never found God.' You reply from your deathbed, 'Sovereign, come and look at me.' Signora, upon my honor, I look into the eyes of undeath only to find the face of my maker."

Near midnight the light through the apse turned to an unsettling shade of blue vapor. He was still smelling smoke, though he had extinguished the prayer candles hours ago. He undid the simple iron latch on the tabernacle. The door fell open of its own accord and he cupped his hands to catch her head, but it did not drop out. He put his hands inside.

"Come," he said.

Then the moon turned its face from the earth and all was darkness, the darkness he'd wished for, disdaining prayer. The silk of the veil was so sheer as to be spectral, though he felt, to his astonishment, a succession of stitched rubrics sewn into the cloth, as of the coverings of the Turk's harem girls in their purdah. This was a sin of mere ignorance, he told her, lifting her out with one hand cupped under her chin and the other supporting her skull. He would do something about it in the morning. Wasn't it time she had a new bedspread, anyway? He brought her to the center of the sacristy and raised her toward the apse. The tail of her veil breezed against his forehead and he thought to bring her down and kiss the crown of her head as well, and he would have had he known when the climax was coming. At the resumption of moonlight, he would jettison her cloak with a swinging motion of his arms and look her full in the face, the tenderness of his almond eyes meeting the bottomless pity of hers, whatever shade they might be ordained to be, and the scars of his rampant adolescent acne coupling with her pockmarks like either end of a severed poem. He waited and waited and the darkness did not lift. He held his breath, daring God, but did not ultimately want to meet the signora in the next world, red-faced and with bulging eyes. When he let out his breath, he heard a sleeper's expiatory moan of horror and he was entirely certain that it was not he who had made the sound. The dew rose on both his palms and warm, salty raindrops slashed down his cheeks.

"Devil!" he cried in the throes of a horror he did not know his system was capable of and swung the skull in the air, warding off her ghost with the cudgel of her own head. He darted back toward the tabernacle, but misjudged and went wide to the right. The ghost's opalescent visage reared out of the darkness, looked with great concern into his eyes, and then butted him with the shell of the stone wig that she wore perhaps, he thought in a flash, as a hedge against a crash-landing. He staggered blindly, rammed the altar, and felt for the tabernacle. He located it and deposited the head. He threw the latch and ran for the exit. The moonlight came up upon a tongue of faded green silk, caught in the crack beneath the tabernacle door, and on the marble Madonna to the right of the sacristy, rocking gently back and forth on her heels.

---

Bernstein kicked up out of the tone poem, a viola on his heels, whole notes dripping from his hair and eyelashes, and caught sight of himself in the Magnavox console at the foot of the bed. Thank God, he thought because his reflection proved that he was no longer the young man he had just been in the dream. Gone were the pretty-boy gangster looks, and safe and sound above his neck was the sedimentary face of the Shanghaied Swami of Moghar of the Buck Rogers serial—probably only extant now in the minds of fond middle-aged men like Lenny—who replied, "Ugh," whenever anyone asked him the meaning of life. In the dream, he was in a room full of people, a New York rent social or an interior fishing expedition on behalf of Tanglewood perhaps, and they were all either turning away when he spoke or regarding him with the eyes of a sturgeon looking up from the supper china. He made jokes at his own expense, gossiped about his more famous friends, played Fats Waller on the baby grand, and the only thing that warmed to him the entire night was the sandpaper of his starched shirt. Was he the main course for the upcoming dinner and was the cold front meant to slowly cook him inside his suit? Envy, anti-Semitism, the stilted demeanors of the knowingly inferior—he never got any of that anymore. Arriving at the Kunstlerhaus three evenings ago, all he had to do was to give the bronze Beethoven in the lobby a whack on the behind and the assembled patricians and the monkey-suited bellhops beamed back their love. And another thing, why always Sibelius at the tail end of dreams?

His secretary Miss Helen Coats hadn't forgotten to pack the crossword sections of five separate international papers (English, German, French, Spanish, and Italian), nor the L&Ms, nor the pertinent and the odd among the correspondences he'd received this week. She also included a driblet from the Sunday *Times*—he read it on the plane—concerning the fictitious rift between himself and Berlin Philharmonic conductor Herbert von Karajan, likening them to two warring popes in an era of history almost entirely lost on Lenny since it predated the development of symphonic music. Humbug, thought Bernstein. Karajan was across town at the Bristol (the man was an Edwardian with a Prussian accent) right now and if the hour wasn't so severe he'd ring him up for a dinner date. There wouldn't be time anyway and their secretaries would cross wires with conflicting excuses for the cancellation. The dinner date would evaporate like a breath mint, leaving the air between the two men artificially sweet. Like a hundred times before.

Earlier in the evening, he had pretty much completed the crosswords, cheating with the paper accordion of his Berlitz Multilingual. He red-penciled his way, once again, through the *Linz* and the *Prague* symphonies as well as the *Violin Sonata in B-flat K. 454;* Isaac Stern was in the air over the Atlantic and Mozart was turning two hundred and eighteen in his early grave. He went to the console and switched on the radio. Mozart, what else? The *Serenata Notturna,* what else? Listening to it, he was reminded of how Felicia had decorated the west room of their new home at the Dakota in New York with seashells—bleached white shells on mantels in glass cases tinted a tranquil blue almost as though they were floating in a joint nebula of moon and sea and clawed and pink-hearted shells along the walls, rimming the entire room. He'd gone in one evening with a cluttered mind while working on *Dybbuk,* his new ballet. He returned to the music room and completed an unconnected five-minute prelude in five minutes, an ocean in miniature.

This week's selected correspondence was bound with a note from Miss Coats. She reminded him of what was contained in which bag, noting with care the location of his inhaler—in with the toiletries—and of how much of which prescription to take, and what not to take with alcohol if he did not wish to return to New York packed in luggage himself. The envelope and the stationery of the first letter on the stack were of a coarse, lusterless provincial paper and he had to put on his half-moon glasses (woe to him who snapped his picture with these granny-annie eyes on) to read the handwriting. The letter was from one Caterina di Siena. There were salutations and congratulations, and then she took grave issue with the Papal Concert he had conducted in Rome a few months ago. First of all, why the *Requiem Mass in D?* Who was it that had died? And couldn't he have chosen a Catholic mass, or at least the work of a "devout Lutheran" such as J. S. Bach? In addition, there was the more serious issue of his hand signals.

*Pardon me, Maestro, for noticing, but during the violin part in the Dies irae you issued the number three with your left hand. At the succeeding violin break in the Rex tremendae, you gave evidence of the number five with a rather placating wave at the fiddle section. Again, with the trombone solo in the Tuba Mirum, you did extend four fingers from your left hand while pronging your baton between the two forefingers of your right hand, thus giving evidence of the number seven. Given your background and your legendary love of both musical and social subversion, I can only conclude that you were speaking in a sort of Cabalistic*

*sign language, each number corresponding to the Sefirot, the ten
supposed emanations of God the Father. Sir, you had the Pope
present, did you also wish to provoke the presence of the Almighty? Or perhaps the Other whose name is an affliction upon
the tongue? Mozart, gracious Maestro, trifled with Zoroastrian
riddles, but he was in blessed ignorance of the stratagems of the
Sephardic Black Book. Did you really think a Papal Concert was
the time and the place?*

    *I await your reply and explanation.*

        *Yours in God,*
        *Caterina di Siena*

She supplied three different return addresses: the house in Siena
where she grew up, the church in the same city where her head
resided, and the one in Rome where her body lay.

What time was it in America and whom could he call about
this? This was priceless. Why hadn't Miss Coats said anything?
He had the phone in his hand before he knew what he was
going to do with it. Its purring was as noxious a warning as
the discord of the alarm clock, but he simply had to tell someone. Obviously, the smartest little girl or boy in some middle-
American schoolroom vacationed in Rome last summer and
witnessed his Papal Concert. She/he fell desperately in love with
Lenny and this was, of course, nothing new. Oh, the adulation
he received care of CBS by virtue of the *Young People's Concerts*
program, impacted flowers, rhyming verse, pressed cotton underwear, the whole bit, the letters always straightforward,
shameless and always begging an answer and an eight-by-ten
glossy. But just look at the way this little boy/girl employed psychology, musicology, history, and Cabalism—a little Mozart was
in love and desperate to make contact with him. Just check this
out, Herbert.

Herbert? The phone grew hot in his hand and he snapped it
back in its cradle. But Karajan was the one who would understand, no doubt. Hadn't they both suffered from the same distor-
tion of sycophancy, the same worshipful hall of mirrors? How

refreshing it was to at last find combative love in this context. Like when he first met Felicia.

Surely, there would be some buffer between his phone line and Karajan's, some aide in an anteroom or, for all he knew (he discounted rumor), a valet sleeping on the phone-friendly side of the bed; von Karajan would have a gentleman's choice whether or not to accept his call. He dialed the operator.

"Operator, liebling, put me through to the Bristol."

She said, "Yes, sir," and he heard the call go through.

"Bristol."

"Yes, please, get me Maestro Karajan's suite. This is Leonard Bernstein calling."

"It is four in the morning."

"You're a switchboard operator, not a clock. Get me Karajan."

The line rang and it was picked up immediately. The Bristol switchboard person said, "Herr Karajan, please. It's a Mister Leonard Bernstein calling."

The aide or valet on the other end began to breathe hard and Bernstein was going to say, "Get me your master," in a sweet, vacant tone like an alien's "Take me to your leader," but he hadn't time for self-deception now. The rattled breath on the line was that of a thirty-year three-pack-a-day man, just like Lenny. When did aides or valets to great men have time to burn sixty cigarettes per day? Across the city, the world's two greatest conductors were orbiting in the same dense silence, each of them controlling it, four masterful hands at the helm.

"Maestro," Bernstein said, "I got a letter from Saint Catherine of Siena."

Karajan said, "Ugh," in the exact cadence of the Shanghaied Swami of Moghar—Buck Rogers in Weimar Germany, that explains the V-2 rocket system, by God!—and he hung up the phone.

---

Lenny lay on the bed, regarding the eggshell tempura pattern of the ceiling, smoking, desperate to get back to the dream—to salvage something from these hours of insomniac limbo. He was going to give the room of surly partygoers the great what-for. Mozart, on the radio, helped ease the transition, and before he knew it he was back at the gathering. Hadn't he noticed a buffet of fruit last time? Yes, there in the corner, ripe and lonely as a bunch of harlots at a cotillion. The partygoers welcomed his return with squinty eyes and signals for more cordials. He pigged his eyes back at them: bright, black-haired Lenny, Koussevitzky's elbow-rest and heir, scion of the tattle columns, and the man who would perennially play the young Tchaikovsky in an upcoming Paramount production. His social life was but an extension of his covenant with God and who could deny the miracle? He was hobnobbing here in the big town while his Russian cousins wire-walked one infraction away from the Soviet camps and millions of his coreligionists were still legible in the hazy script over the Vistula River. He crossed to the buffet table, picked up a halved Neapolitan orange, and stared into its bloody viscera. "Alas, poor Yorick," he said and squeezed the fruit's red guts out onto the floor. The room took a breath and exhaled in laughter. Karajan never got a laugh like that in his life.

---

The rabble queued at the chapel gates in the early morning dark and, arriving to say mass, Father Burgio could only conclude that the Black Plague and its attendant fear of God had returned to Siena after an absence of five-hundred years. No one came in for the service, but for the Vacco sisters who made up his core morning congregation, and the Father grew suspicious and went out to the steps during the Kyrie eleison.

"Well, what do you all want?" he asked them.

"The job," they said as one, and Burgio remembered the "night watchman needed" blurb Father Rizzolo inserted into last week's newsletter. Burgio hadn't minded being upstaged by sleep and complacency, but playing second banana to menial employment was intolerable. He turned back to the Vacco sisters, who were warbling through the Kyrie in faltering harmony, and said, "Church dismissed!"

Father Rizzolo interviewed them one after the other. They

were mostly youths tangibly older than he because their child-hoods had been their primes. They were still living in the vacu-ums of their father's houses and contemplating the move to Milan or Rome or the transmigration to America—an improb-ability ingrained in their bloodstreams now. They saw lofty gran-deur in soft employment and working in the chapel was at least something their mothers could brag about over coffee. There was one job for the three hundred of them and Rizzolo wondered why they didn't work harder to make an impression. He wasn't accepting resumes—what credentials could he ask for?—but these dullards, who sat there in their imitation-silk printed shirts with wrist and chest hairs blooming, begrudged him even their ages and names, and seemed baffled when he asked of their em-ployment histories. Perhaps he should choose the biggest, hairi-est among them, or conduct an olfactory survey and select the most fetid, the greatest stranger to the deodorant aerosol. It would serve Catherine right.

Father Rizzolo's hand was tender from the day's endless "How do you do's" and he was relieved that the little man with the low tide hairline, the saint's worried eyes, the attaché case, and the permanent-press suit shook hands as feyly as a cat. He gave his name as Massimo La Rocca and his profession as "musical secretary."

"Do you mean that you were a secretary to a conductor?" Riz-zolo ventured.

"And a composer as well."

"And what came between yourself and this sort of work?"

"My master decomposes," said La Rocca.

The prefect heard his own laughter rinsing the vaulted arch above his head and he saw it reflected in the faces of the remain-ing youths in the dwindling line. As though priests were not al-lowed laughter.

"Mr. La Rocca," he said, "what do you know of Catherine of Siena?

"That she needs someone."

A German named Mauer came to Siena many years past to deal in rare books and befriend local men who did not particularly enjoy his friendship; it was a dirty job, and someone had to get paid for it. Rizzolo, liking his company and not minding his pre-dilections (the Bible itself equivocated the issue), wrote letters of introduction on his behalf to clerics and prelates, and members of the threadbare nobility who might happen to have ancestral libraries to sell. Mauer died at his desk, licking a stamp, and his widow—a northern blonde whom he married in order to have someone to introduce at cocktail parties—found him slumped forward with his tongue lolling out. She amused herself by past-ing the stamp to her husband's forehead with the last of his saliva and then she phoned Rizzolo. He organized the funeral, gave the eulogy, and evidenced saintliness in the behavior of the widow's thirteen-year-old daughter Sabrina, whom he had only glimpsed and nodded hello to previously. He was newly burdened with free time, owing to Catherine's rejection, and he offered to free her from the spirit-crushing public school system. He would tu-tor her, gratis of course—Mauer hadn't consummated his mar-riage, hadn't fathered Sabrina, and hadn't left them a red piastra.

Sabrina was one of those rare children who loved school, the solicitude of the teachers who adored her, the companionship of the little girls, and the airsickness she was beginning to affect upon the little boys. She had a gentle spirit, all told, but she hated Rizzolo and his habit of chiding her for her forgetfulness with a pat under the chin. She was blonde like her mother and very often, while he read aloud to her from Petrarch or Saint Thomas of Aquino, she would sweep her hair over her face and stare at him through the adornment of gold, willing him into a pig's tail and later a pubic strand, the two possibilities she thought best suited his personality. He obstinately refused to change form and he left off noticing when she hid under her hair. She lost patience and waited for that hand to chuck her jawbone one more time. When it finally did, she snarled and bit him be-tween the knuckles with sharp incisors, which, in later adoles-cence, would prove themselves in the snapping of key rings and the cracking of lobster shells. The lightning thrill of it ran up his forearm and detonated an electric charge in his funny bone. He found himself waving goodbye to his core belief of celibacy, strictly speaking, and he extended the other hand.

"Do it again, damn you," he said and she did.

She warmed to him under the spell of these biting sessions; it was her first real taste of the carnal authority that she was born with and that had slept in gestation inside her all along. If she wanted to skip the day's geometry lesson, for instance, all she had to do was to threaten not to bite him and he would relent. He went about in black velvet gloves, allowing to anyone who asked that God was testing him with late-blooming eczema. Also, in cataloging Mauer's holdings as a favor to the widow, he found a cache of Asian child porn done in lithography—Buddha figures straddling prepubescent girls with comely and cruel reptilian features so like that of the changeling in Christus's *Portrait of a Lady*. Looking at the prints through his jeweler's monocle, he reminded himself that it was the indulgent God who'd given grace to the early Renaissance and the revived Old Testament patriarch who had sullied it; witness those Botticellis on the bonfires. He was sure to take off his white collar and gold cross before he pleasured himself.

Then he got a letter about it, a prank letter on Santo Domenico stationery of all things and actually signed with the willful blasphemy of Catherine's name. He found it folded in the pocket of his black coat as he retrieved it from the church's rack one evening. It detailed everything—the masochistic indulgences with Sabrina, the Dowager Empress–era kid porn, and the furtive self-adjustments in the attic closet. Who could have known? Who at the chapel? Father Burgio was deaf and myopic and spent whole afternoons in moral dispute with the whore of Babylon. The sexton could not write his name, let alone an admonishing, Catherinesque letter. La Rocca, the night man, would sit in the front pew doodling musical notations and humming to himself, and Rizzolo often thought that if the chapel should cave in around him he would mark the occasion with perhaps a dart of his eye. It was not inconceivable that his name was being bantered about in relation to a bishop's office, and self-styled devil's advocates were known to reap muck in such an instance, but all the letter threatened him with was the forfeiture of his immortal soul; there was not a hint of earthly blackmail in its pristine prose. It was Catherine, herself—it just had to be. He heard all his life of the wrath of a woman scorned, and one of life's deepest lessons, he knew from his studies, was that there was verisimilitude in the hoariest of old clichés, such as the interventions of the saints.

He was not a praying man, despite his vocation. All his life he addressed Catherine in the Santo Domenico as though she were merely the person sitting across the room from him. Now he found himself on his knees, alone in his room, speaking properly to her in Latin (surely she had learned the language in the afterworld) and begging her to leave him alone and allow him to be the man he always dreamed he could be. The reply he wished for was total silence, but this was not to be. He received two more reprimanding letters, one in his eyeglass case and the other stuck in the sweatband of his bowler. If praying was to no avail, the matter had to be taken in hand. He went by railway to Florence and picked up a mannequin's head and a leaden strongbox at a flea market. He wrapped the mannequin's head in plain cotton swaddling cloth and put it inside the strongbox. When Massimo La Rocca arrived for work the following evening, Rizzolo sent him home, saying he wished to pray alone through the night. He sat in the front pew with the strongbox in his lap and waited for the appropriate midnight.

---

Bernstein napped before the performance and didn't have time to go over the rehearsal notes. He woke and dressed leisurely, knowing better than to ruin the hush of the precelestial mood by rushing. It was foolish to worry anyway. The Vienna Philharmonic knew Mozart, to be sure, and although he hadn't seen Isaac Stern, the man was booked, so where else could he be? He stepped out of the dressing room and walked down the darkened corridor toward the light of the Konzerthaus Theater. In the wings three assistants approached him. One lit an L&M and pressed it to his lips, another followed by cupping the plastic yarmulke of an oxygen mask over his mouth, and the last gave him a petting with a portable garment vacuum.

"Say, where's Stern?" he let slip and the three assistants acted as though they hadn't heard. He stepped into the light and row after row sprung up and applauded. Lenny loved it, reveled in it, and deep in his heart he was scared to death of it—four, five thousand people auditing his every move night after night—anybody from anywhere as long as they had evening clothes and the price of admission. He'd worked and studied and plotted his whole life first to get into this room and then to be able to return to it each season, no small feat for a Jew from Lawrence, Massachusetts. Some of the older ones in attendance tonight had adulated Hitler—who knows, perhaps in this same hall.

The concertmaster brought him a leather-bound copy of the score—a custom in Vienna—and Bernstein had a crisis of short-term memory. He'd been rehearsing the orchestra for the better part of a week, but he had no memory of ever laying eyes on this man before. He knew better than to let on, but, instead, grasped the man's hand and gave him his messianic look—a look as frank as the gaze of a lover, but one that said not "I love you," but "You will love me." The El Greco eyes of the short, dark, balding man betrayed nothing and Bernstein turned up the heat and met his own face, deep in the acidic pond of the man's stomach. Something was very wrong here. He'd known musicians all his life and this man was none. This man was as vacant as the angel of death. Lenny's eyes grazed the cover of the score. It said, "*Requiem Mass in D* by Wolfgang Amadeus Mozart," whereas it was supposed to be a copy of the *Linz Symphony*. He smelled a prank: a fake concertmaster and the wrong score. The Philharmonic was priming him for a practical joke. Tranquil old Vienna loved a belly laugh dearly. He could see it in the musicians' faces now. The undue tension, the coiled stillness—they were waiting to pin him with donkey ears. He would give them their cue and the Philharmonic would caterwaul or play some absurdly orchestrated version of "Mary Had a Little Lamb."

There was nothing to do but to play along. It was terrible manners to outwit a joke, after all. He reached into the lining pocket of his tux and removed his baton, fashioned from the wood of an olive tree planted on the day Israel declared its statehood. He tapped the lectern, made eye contact all around, and then, unsure whether to give an up or a down beat, he mimed a parting of invisible curtains. He knew from the first notes—that strange enigmatical river, the sound painting in Lenny's mind of Ophelia billowing through the rushes—this could only be Mozart's unfinished farewell poem. The last time he conducted the *Requiem Mass,* a pope had wept. But where was the joke? What was so amusing about switching the *Linz* for the *Requiem* and willfully confusing the conductor? Shouldn't he at least make a pretense of being angry? Karajan would be hurling chairs by now.

The choir sang in the loft above his head. He was weak with incomprehension and afraid that he would swoon. But—goddamn!—this did make sense, after all, there was indeed a jest in all of this and Lenny was the only one in on it. What could be funnier than the indefatigable Lenny grown old and senile? He'd woken from his nap thinking he was fourteen years younger. That *Linz* and *Prague* concert was long ago. The true date was January 27, 1988, and Leonard was jointly conducting the Vienna Philharmonic with the ailing Karajan tonight to commemorate Mozart's two hundred and thirty-second birthday. How the world had changed in the space of one nap. Felicia dead of cancer—what, ten years now? The home movies, the correspondence, and a room filled with seashells to remember her by. His children grown and married; one grandchild in the world and another in the making. The man he'd left Felicia for withering of AIDS back in New York. Only the music remained young.

The funniest part of it was that he, the world's foremost conductor (the arthritic, eighty-year-old Karajan was a crippled marionette now), was so surprised that he was powerless to do anything with this music. The best he could manage was to fan his arms and grin like a borscht belt comic doing Toscanini—it was conducting him. The hollow places he'd held back from forty years of psychotherapy—old grudges, guilts and jealousies—provided the fossil fuel and he did not resist, and no one even seemed discomfited when his Italian heels levitated off of the platform and Lenny began his orbit. In the upper galleries, they were laughing along with him. He treaded air, improvised a pirouette, and heard cries of "moonvalk!" and "Villy Jean is not my loover!" The plaster cherubs in the ceiling giggled and pointed; Lenny curled into a fetal ball, tumbling end over end for the sheer infantile joy of it; jeweled hands reached over the balconies to touch him as he rolled by. For years, critics had accused him of upstaging the music by dancing and leaping at the lectern. He couldn't wait to read their grousing about this new flying business.

Then it hit him. He veered, breakneck, around a column at the back of the hall and he knew in an instant that he was not going to live through this, his ash canister lungs would no doubt dissolve in a minute or two. He would belch black soot and careen to the parquet below. What the hell, though, instant eulogies, his three symphonies, his dances, suites and songs on every quality radio station in the world, and flags of every stripe at half-staff. Pity he wouldn't be around to see it, but he had another engagement. He had another audience as well. The Almighty had had His eye on Bernstein for a very long time and at last He was reaching out His palm. He wanted God to know that it was all right with him. Given his preference, he'd die while doing Mahler back at Avery Fisher and he would have assuredly drawn up an alternative guest list, but then again it was kind of a blessing not to be saddled with such details. Sailing, Lenny threw up his hands to the heavens. Okay by Bernstein.

He held two fingers in the air to signal the Hokmah, the second emanation of Jehovah, which was His attribute of unfathomable wisdom, as he remembered Israeli Philharmonic musicians, as well as their audience, doing during a tremor in the desert so many years ago. In the middle of an open-air concert, Shostakovich evaporated and he heard a subterranean roaring that came and went like a thunderstorm, fraying only nerves. Presently, a wit in the upper tier of the Viennese theater wondered aloud if Lenny wasn't gesturing for a bathroom break. He laughed along with the audience and signaled the remaining potencies of God in no particular order, and then all of the possible combinations of these potencies so that his conversation with his maker degenerated into mathematical gibberish—a mad prayer in a deaf language. There were other preparations. It was gauche to die with your clothes on, no? He'd come into the world in no tuxedo. Hovering over the orchestra, he loosened his bow tie and dropped it down the spout of a French horn. The glazed, oxygen-deprived eyes of the brass section, the contorted heads of the violinists—he'd never noticed such things before. Beauty was hard work, wasn't it? Dying should be so hard, thought Lenny as he kicked off his boots and wriggled out of his trousers. There would be a certain justice if dying were as difficult as being born.

He flew over the concertmaster and his suspicions were confirmed; the man played no instrument. He sat there jotting musical notes onto a loose-leaf pad. He caught his eye—death's dark eye—and curled his upper lip, but the man only looked back to the notebook and continued his scribbling. He rose to the choir loft just as the singers widened their mouths to begin the Hostias. He singled out a plump, broad-shouldered matron with cold, ultramarine eyes. Staring her down, he mentally provided her with a commandant's uniform and a leather whip. He removed his silken boxers and the matron stretched her jaw and aimed a jagged aural lightning bolt directly at him. Lenny dodged it, light as a wasp.

"Say ahh, baby," he said and flew on.

Rizzolo didn't wear a watch; he calculated that it was near to midnight by the color of the moonlight through the apse and by the complete drainage of his patience. He said a four-word prayer, "Father, I am ashamed," and went to the tabernacle. He took out Catherine's cloth-covered head without looking at it and pretended to himself that he could not feel the mold of her cranium through the black lace gloves he wore even in the bath now. He replaced her head with the mannequin's in its shroud and dropped the genuine Catherine into the strongbox he'd picked up in Florence. He locked up the church and set out for the Ombrone River.

Arriving, he recognized something strange in the current—it lurched noncommittally, almost spasmodically, like an animal with a broken resolve. He washed his face in the cold water and looked up at the moon with needles in his eyes. The moon falsified into a face; it was her face, there was no mistaking Sodoma's broad-cheeked, almost Flemish vision of her. He had never been drunk in his life, but he guessed that this was what inebriation must be like, a private theater wherein the heart's dark wishes were cast as characters and objective reality was subordinated to the status of stage props. He addressed the moon.

"So, you love me after all. No? Will you deny it? If I'm just an ordinary man to you, why did you come back to life? Why did you spy on me? Why did you leave those letters inside my coat? Why would you care? I worshipped you for years and you never gave me a single sign. I fall out of love with you and you're in my coat, you're in my eyeglasses, you're in my hat. Don't think I don't understand, I wrote a dissertation on you, after all. There is one quality you love in a man and it isn't that saintliness you preached in those letters—you love aloofness, signora. You loved it in Jesus and you love it in me. I know how painful it is to love the dead, but I truly cannot imagine your agony, the dead in love with the living. I won't let you. No, I will not let you imprison your immortal, beatified, canonized soul in a gilded cage. Catherine, I kill you only out of caring."

The moon was the moon again and he had not yet bidden her goodbye. She was hiding in that moon, slyly delaying the inevitable. Was he man enough? Had his vows emasculated him or did he possess enough residual virility to take the head from its wrappings? Could he bid her farewell face-to-face, as all lovers must if they are ever to be allowed to love again? He opened the strongbox and tore at the cloth with his eyes closed. The chill penetrated even the gloves as he raised the head high—where he knew the beam of the moon would be. He opened his eyes and looked into a face straight out of an American horror film. She had a monk's circled pate of close-cropped hair; it stood straight up like wheat and it was as green as young corn. Her skin was a blotchy paraffin hidebound to the bones of her face— the prominent pox scars giving her complexion the look of Swiss cheese. She had the eyes of Medusa, filmed-over and inquiring into infinity. Her lips were curled into the white of her gums and she snarled at him with her three remaining front teeth. Her legend was correct, she had to be a saint, with a face like that she was fit only for the love of God. He threw her head in the river and turned and kicked the strongbox, crushing his toe. He hobbled home with his priest's collar in his mouth, chewing it like taffy.

She came up in a fishing net the next morning and she was in the papers by evening. LEPER'S HEAD FOUND IN THE OM-BRONE, the headlines read. Paul VI sent condolences and concerns and offered up masses for the repose of the leper woman's soul. The press printed her photograph and offered substantial rewards for information leading to the total annihilation of whoever it was that killed her. In the taverns, however, they dubbed it a mercy killing and drank to her death. Leaden jokes made the rounds. Rizzolo himself might have laughed if he had been in any mood for irony. He drafted and redrafted his suicide note and lived from newspaper to newspaper as the investigators canvassed sanitariums as far away as Palermo, offending these institutions with leading questions about runaway patients. Lab tests proved that the woman had been dead for some time—years even. The grave robbing angle reared its head in the newspapers, and cranks phoned the police departments, turning in their brother-in-laws and next-door neighbors. Rizzolo, more than once, dissolved rat poison in glasses of grappa, toasted Catherine, and lost his nerve as the tumbler touched his lips. Then a local dentist and his wife came forward, claiming that the head belonged to their Atalanta. Years ago she abandoned their home, leaving only a note of apology for having disgraced the family, and they took Atalanta to mean that she had gotten herself pregnant, not that she had contracted an archaic skin disease. Only now did they allow themselves to cry over her. The authorities hastily believed their story and the matter was put to rest, along with the head, in the garden abutting the Palazzo Pubblico.

Rizzolo went incognito to confession in another parish. He volunteered everything except his identity and the disbelieving voice on the other end of the screen said, "So, you're clear for this life. What about after?"

"Tell me my penance," he droned like a clerk in a records office soliciting the date of yet another inconsequential birth.

The voice answered, "I'm sorry, that's out of my jurisdiction."

Rizzolo vowed to take his case to a higher authority.

---

Lenny landed in a shower of roses, his naked belly doing its merry little harem jig as the final note of the *Requiem* blissed out into silence—but where was death? His intended climax had gotten away from him; a matter of over-rehearsal, he supposed. He had never noticed before how staccato applause sounded, no matter how many hands were clapping. What an incredibly ugly way of saying thanks. What's more, they all looked as habituated as circus seals. How about a few tears? He shivered and one of the aides came out with a dressing gown. The clapping pounded in his temples and the somber little concertmaster put aside his notebook and got up from his chair. Here it comes. They were stomping in the aisles. What more could they want, his death? He was too exhausted to put up a fight, but he wasn't going to give up without a joke. From five feet away, the concertmaster extended his hand for a shake. Lenny thought fast. He held up one hand for silence and with the other he staved off the figure of death in the ill-fitting tux. Vienna quieted and listened. Bernstein leaned to the microphone and whispered, "Heil Hitler," and five thousand concertgoers turned to the aisle, as one. Over their shoulders, they heard the sound of Leonard Bernstein laughing alone.

That oughta hold them. He turned to take the dark angel's hand. He found himself gripping something cylindrical and slender and he looked down to find a ballpoint in his palm. The concertmaster extended his notebook. In a heavy Tuscan accent, he said, "Laney, I gotta have-a you autograph."

---

Rizzolo wrote letters, did favors, pleaded, and pulled strings. Prayer was out of the question. Years passed and he was finally given minor curatorial duties at the Vatican; his job was to transfer the written files concerning the relics of the saints onto microfiche. It seemed the more obscure the saint was, the more minor the body part would be—tibia of Saint Elias of Waziristan, for instance. In his lonely cubicle, he daydreamed of attaching all of the bones specified in the files and creating a "supersaint" or a Catholic Golem. His dark gloves aroused suspicion, but he pleaded his eczema as well as the delicate nature of his work. His promised invitation to the Pope's apartments for Sunday dinner was postponed many times—this although he had shadowed His Holiness on his evening walks and he once saw him eating fried squid with tourists along the Spanish stairs. He borrowed money and bought several meat berths from a departing slaughterhouse, and then donated them to a local orphanage to be converted into bunk beds, bragging his deed around the office until everyone knew that there was but one way to get him to be quiet about it. He received an invitation written in gold lettering on marbleized paper.

---

The Pontiff entered from his private rooms with Massimo La Rocca, dressed as a Jesuit. Massimo had a sharpened pencil behind his ear and although Rizzolo thought that he was prepared for anything, this was anything but anything. The little night man at the Santo Domenico? He'd bid him goodbye in Siena not three years ago and it takes longer to become a Jesuit than it does to become a doctor of medicine. Rizzolo gasped, "La Rocca?" and La Rocca turned and looked at John Paul.

"What's that in Italian, Your Holiness?" he said in English.

"Fortress, Carl," John Paul said. "Rocks they built the church on."

La Rocca's twin, whom the Pope called Carl, extended his hand. "Thanks," he said. He changed his mind when Rizzolo reached with his black glove. "I'll wait until your rash heals, fella," said La Rocca.

"Father Carl is American, " the Pope said. "And you are?"

"Italian."

"No, you are who?"

"Father Rizzolo."

"Father Rizzolo, do you know that Father Carl has revolutionized something as ancient as prayer. He takes my conversations with God, writes them down, and he translates them into music, the alphabet corresponding to the major and minor scales. While I am sleeping, he goes into the chapel and plays my prayers on the organ. Just in case God did not hear the first time."

The conversation around the dinner table was Epicurean in nature—the Pope's inner circle droning on about flavorsome wines and elitist inns hewn into the rock in the hills above Rome. The Pope said very little and even his smile seemed superfluous; there was such an air of beneficence about him that Rizzolo was beginning to believe in halos, psychic ones anyway. He forgot everything he was going to say and this was to the good; his silence ingratiated him with the Pontiff, and then John Paul looked at him over his roast beef—none of that Asiatic vegetarian nonsense for this old shipyard hand—and said, "What is it you do for us, again, Father?"

Rizzolo said, "Your Holiness, I deal with the bones of great souls."

"That is a noble undertaking."

"Undertaking?"

John Paul didn't get it for a half an instant. When he laughed, the rest of the table laughed as well.

"And has your vocation given you any insights into human nature?"

"Only that the outer shells are hard and that the marrow is dry."

This time they laughed without the Pontiff's help. John Paul looked around for more wine. At the height of the laughter, Rizzolo slipped off his black glove and put his right hand into his finger bowl. The ringworm mementos of Sabrina's teeth, from knuckles to wrist, were scarred in a pattern vaguely resembling the astronomical symbol of the moon in its last quarter. The table quieted instantly.

"Stigmata," someone whispered.

John Paul was the last to notice and he spent an uncomfortable interval searching through the pockets of his robes for his bifocals. He put them on, leaned close, drew back, and then nudged Massimo's look-alike. Rizzolo looked into the Pontiff's careworn face—a slept-in bed, newly vacated and warm, yes, so warm that you could put your palm to it and read the temperature of its dreams.

"Make a note of that, will you?" the Pope said.

Father Carl wrote something on a napkin and put it into his pocket. This was it; at most he'd have to spend a hundred or two hundred years windsurfing the cosmos with the unbaptized fetuses of Limbo while the sanctification process moved forward in God's own time, but not even God could condemn a verified saint. He'd let King David, the adulterer and homicide-conspirator, off the celestial hook, hadn't he? Anyway, his indiscretions with Saint Catherine of Siena had happened during his unbridled youth and he drowned her dead skull rather than consummate anything. He dried his hand and put his glove back on.

"Pardon me, Your Holiness."

"Of course," John Paul said. "Now who do I have to beatify to get a glass of wine around here?"

---

Bernstein showered and went across the hall in his robe—sandal tongues flapping, parched white shins gleaming—to Karajan's dressing room in order to apologize. He'd scared away the gala audience and served Mozart a hollow birthday cake. He rapped at the door and there was no answer. He called, in falsetto, "Maestro! Oh, Maestro!" Still no answer. He turned the doorknob. Aristocrats don't bother with locked doors. Bernstein was born middle-class and many years ago, at the initial flush of *Fancy Free* and *On the Town* fame, he learned the first lesson in the psychology of money when total strangers began to hit him up for loans in nightclubs—there is no hiding and green is not the color of camouflage. Karajan was born knowing that, no doubt. He tasted champagne in the womb and arrived punctually, though naked and squalling, at a cocktail party given in his honor. The door popped open, as Lenny anticipated, and Ben Gay hung in the air, thick and blue as cigarette smoke in the movies. Karajan stood at the washbasin, the Konzerthaus being over three hundred years old and the installing of showers having been in committee for thirty years. The old maestro was stripped to the waist and the sight of him had Lenny wondering if Giacometti ever sculpted in white marble.

"Maestro, I—"

"Leenny, this medicine is not vorking."

Karajan's hands trembled over the basin, the tap roaring, water pounding the tin bottom. The unguent waxed his knuckles—those hands, those Nazi fellow-traveler's rabbinical hands. There was a hundred-year-old Rebbe he knew in Brooklyn who couldn't claim to have once delineated God with the power of Karajan.

"You want to wash it off?" Bernstein asked.

"Yes. But I'm afraida za pain. Imagine, at my age."

"Chrissake, let me help you."

He crossed the room and cooled both the rush and the fever of the tap. He took the maestro by the fingers.

"We're going to go slow. Let me know if you want to stop."

Karajan flinched at the touch of the water, but said nothing. Lenny felt it dampen the hem of his robe, a trickle running down his leg. He caught sight of himself and his friend and rival in the oval mirror above the basin. The maestro was grimacing and Bernstein smiled so as to complete the tragicomic emblem.

Karajan said, "Leenny, vill ve ever die?"

"Why do you ask that? Is the pain that bad?"

"No. I vant to zee God."

Lenny said, "Why don't you look in the mirror?"

**Ice Age**    The grate above her was half a city block in diameter; the rusted horseshoe lock was as big as a chimney; the smelting plant across the field operated night and day, and neither the noise nor the metallic dust ever ceased. When she thrashed upon the floor, trying to sleep, she created dark angel patterns upon a background of glitz. She answered to the name Electra. It was morning and the breath holes in the grate darkened momentarily—she envisioned stars shimmering. She stood and kicked at the iron dirt. Through the previous night, she had diagrammed the eight positions of the grand pas de Basque, designed a helmet with a sapphire beam for her fairy prince to wear to her rescue, retrieved from memory the opening notes of DJ Gawt Shawt's *Danze Macabre,* and had done a drawing secretly entitled *The Forest at San Miquelon,* which showed a thicket of thin-shanked saplings huddled on a narrow plateau like a boy's choir in a cornice. The twin doors of the grate were axled up by the Norwegian Guard of the Elders, and though there were ten of them for the task, she had ample time to destroy the night's work.

The one with the props was named De Ville; he was the only one who ever spoke to her—the others hovered with crossed arms and chain gold hogdogging the available light. De Ville himself wore no gold, although, in legend, he had appraised the frosted maidenstones that Furio Montagne's conquered harlots adulated G. God Blight with, and in addition to his other titles he bore the honorific "Jeweler to the Honeyman." Electra stood and recited her prison digits. He commanded her to look at him; she looked without hesitation. He wore a sable top hat, which caved forward of its own ungainly stovepipe hollowness, and from where she was standing he held the sun directly between his legs.

He said, "So, wha's up, spoilsport?"

She answered, "Four years, two-hundred-and ninety-two days, seven hours, fifteen minutes—"

"Timepieces be contraband."

"I ain't got no timepiece."

"You sayin' you counted?"

"It's my time, ain't it? I s'pose you don't never count your money."

"I ain't got time," he said, and the four other Elders grunted, and the Norwegians, who were pretty much forbidden facial expressions, smiled, though it appeared that they might only be curling back the fishbone blades of their upper lips.

"What was it you was in for again?" he asked, pretending to have forgotten.

She related the story of her acrylic and mixed media work *Whilst Their Backs Were Turned* exactly as though she were four-one-oneing it for the very time. It was a depiction of the wives of the brethren of the High Elder Protocol Committee and also of the wife of G. God Blight himself. Blight's wife, obese in proportion to the expansion of her husband's renown, was sitting naked upon a vaguely oriental rug, molding small animals with excess portions of her own flesh. De Ville's wife was engaged in rouging her anal opening with blood from the corpse of James Brown, crucified horizontally on a synthesizer nearby. W. D. Dot Com Biz B's wife was behind, on Mrs. De Ville's blind side, holding a lawn dart. The painting had hung for eleven minutes in the unisexual rest room of the Club Voortrekkerhoogte, before being yanked down by an alert patron who, to his credit, offered to buy it when it was reclaimed from the underside of his garment.

"And y'all ain't got no sense of humor, your damn selfs," Electra told the Elders.

"Done anything else?" De Ville asked.

"Nothin' lately."

"And you figure you gonna re-up on the outside?"

"By law."

"Oh, yeah?" Even from far below, she could see his eyebrows rise like synchronized parachutes.

"The judge drummed five times," she said. "Check out my calendar."

She cocked her head to the anthracite wall to her left where she had scratched out four-and-three-fourths x figures with shingled edges like those of the Aryan good luck symbol.

"No say?" De Ville said. "Y'all don't get the morning papers down there, do ya?"

"Contraband."

"I don't know why. In lieu of news, we just print who's nookin' who."

"That's news to me."

"It ain't to me. Even before it happens."

"What you doin', Ville? Breedin' uber-negrons?"

"Shush, that's a secret. What I'm tryin' to tell you is we got a new Act of Parliament. Article eight-trey-eight-aught-seven specifically states that all felonious monks, and likewise shorties, have got to prove their phatness to reenter society."

"How?"

"Got us an exam."

"And I bet its oral."

His laughter amounted to one mirthless convulsion, like someone reacting to a back spasm. He sidelonged the other Elders, who neither laughed nor dared to meet his eye.

"What I say?" he said. "Girl got more spunk than a trey-ball rooster in an egg plant."

"Eggplant?" said Donald Thirty-Eight F. X. Elder, who had not been listening attentively and suspected that he had been called a moolie.

"Naw, girl, it ain't oral and it ain't even verbal. If you want out, you go the way you come."

"Get specific."

"Shore thing," he said and clapped his hands.

She heard an engine turn over and the other Elders slid to the side. A hydraulic limb the color of a canary loomed over the grate, dangling a roof-sized canvas mounted on a hardwood spike. The spike slithered down a length of chain and landed upright in the dirt of her cell. She noticed a palette of premixed oils stapled to the hide of the spike. She braced herself and tugged it free. Bound with a red ribbon to the palette were four painting brushes; she passed her hand over each of them, the bristles thorny and resilient, like the high-ass Astroturf weaves that she remembered as being in vogue in the season before her incarceration.

"That's your tremblin' virgin, 'Lectra," De Ville said. "You go on and wet yo'self up somethin', don't you mind me and the boys a'tall."

"Like what?"

"Up to yourself."

"The shit you say?"

"The shit I don't," he said, fanning his hands. "If we favorable to what you paint, you free on your due date."

"What otherwise?"

"Otherwise, more of the same."

"Like how much more?"

"Say, ten years more."

"Gawd dawg!" she cursed him, sweeping up on her tiptoes. "Whyn't you let a person know aforehand?"

"Huh-uh, shorty," he said and tisked his tongue like an overgrown hamster. "This here is a spot up mind read. It's like Rothschilds."

"That's Rorschach's, landfill head."

"Whatever." He screwed his eyes. "Wasn't no vocab class at the revolution. You better get to wettin'."

She spoked the bushes in the webbed interruptions between her fingers; De Ville remarked to his brother Elders that it looked like she was throwing up some sort of warped-ass gang sign. She stepped to the canvas and peered into its blank face, her brow broke up, she backtracked.

"Damn thing's pure rink," she said. "Am I allowed to touch?"

De Ville hinged forward, slow and steady, his torso finally achieving a ninety over the precipice.

"What?"

"Touch."

"Now, I got to climb all the way down there . . ."

"Wait up," she said. "Each canvas has got an individual character. It ain't one size fit all like that barbershop you go to where all the man got is a chamber pot and a Gillette Superstroke."

"That a fact?" he said, his back now audibly creaking.

Electra could wait no more for permission—she placed her open palm on the center of the canvas in a gesture that was so like shaking hands in the visiting room of a prison. "Cold," she said, her voice locing up to forty-five rpm.

"We keep it in the courtyard." De Ville was busy kneading the small of his spine. "'Til the Transvaal Conference, El Pro Comm's decided to use only blank canvases as decorative art."

"More to the imagination," she told him with the brushes now bundled in her armpit and both her hands tracing circles around the canvas.

"Yeah, well, we got us a revolution to run now, you know? You drawin' a bead on that bad boy?"

"Yeah, I am. It's a big ol' knot of pure cold cupcake with no fillin'. It's like a glacier."

"Well, wet it up."

"Like it's cold here," she said, ignoring him and cutting her eye toward her left hand. "But warmer here." She swiveled her eyes right. "In the warm part, I'm seein' sunshine. Like a gold and amber bloodstream in the transparent flesh of an ice god."

"Go on, then. Paint it."

"I mean to, Ville. Now, in the chill part, I figure a white so blindingly cold, hard, and clustered that it actually looks like a big ol' prehistoric diamond. Damn."

"Okay, but all day ain't no option. Don't you let yo' hands get all iced to that Etch-A-Sketch."

"Hold it, it's warmin' up."

"What you mean, meltin'?"

"Naw, it's more like morphin'."

"Huh?"

"The glacier, it's . . ."

"Say it."

"I can't," she said with her two hands winding around the canvas with the frenzy of two rats running reels.

"Oh-uhm, is there some sort of emergency with you? You look like a knobby tryin' to cop his first feel."

"It's warm under the chill."

"It's tombstone-ass cold up here."

"Leave me be, now."

"Want us to?"

Her hands halted dead center on the canvas.

"De Ville," she said, "this ain't no glacier no more. It's an ice woman. She's cold on the outside and warm all on the in."

"Naw, naw, we ain't talkin' Elders' wives again, are we?"

She started speaking even before he had stopped, her voice a rapid and light vapor.

"She's gold, pale, and pristine, home," she said. "She got dreads like frozen snakes and eyes that roll white as the belly of the moon. Afore Jesus, De Ville."

He waited a moment and then he said, "And I am buh-lack but comely as the curtains of Solomon, as the dead daughters of Jerusalem."

She had not anticipated his knowing the Song of Songs, even in a bastardized form, though evidence of his interest in the occult had long been rumored to her. The story went that he had dispatched G. God Blight's phantom killer with a ruby bullet painted at the tip with a magenta dye so as to eternally mark the murderer's soul—he bragged that he would enter the underworld one day and rekill the first spirit he came upon with a reddish purple rash over his heart. Nevertheless, the throwaway biblical quote parted the golden mist for her and she saw—she did not imagine—her glacial female in the throes of birth labor. She imparted her vision unto De Ville and the other Elders, cold grabbing images from the Song as they rippled through her head.

"The ice woman," said Electra, "got eyes of doves by the rivers of waters, washed with milk and fitly set. She got a neck like a tower of David. Legs like pillars of marble. Titties like clusters of vines."

She then moved beyond mere plagiarism and described her ice woman "limboing backward like Niagara Falls in reverse." She went on to tell them how an actual birth canal opened just below the gulf of the woman's navel and how the smoke of cloistered ice and the howl of the north wind issued forth. The sliver edge of De Ville's tongue was stiff in concentration at the corner of his mouth.

"So, what's the child look like?" he wanted to know.

"Duluth," she said and spat out of the corner of her mouth in disgust at being misunderstood. The foamy pearl of saliva sparkled and dried on the ashen silver floor.

"So," she said, "you send me down a pot of espresso and you put on 'In Tongues' by Avalon and the Avaricious. In a couple of hours, I'll have somethin' that'll stop your soul."

"Yo, 'Lectra," she heard him say and she did not look even as the canvas and its wooden column were levitated away on the steel strings of the crane; neither did she raise her eyes when she felt the presence of two immense shadows on either of her shoulders that hinged forward until they left only a skunk's stripe of light across the very top of her head, and then not even that.

"Dark damn fast this season," she whispered.

He could not have heard her, but he felt his broad shadow displacing the eyelets of light that came through the punch holes in the grate above. She heard him say, "That's good, think of it as winter. Even the earth gets stripped and cold-stored."

"And what is the earth's crime?"

He could not have heard her, but, deep inside her head, she heard him murmur, "Immortality."

He was gone.

———————

Through the first months of her second term, she slept soundly for the most part; her dreams were plotless, but the images in them were long-lasting, like a series of sweet and stately trumpet lines. Her yesterdays were not differentiated from todays, so she saw no choice but to regress. She became infantile to the point of gathering the smoothest stones amid the gravel and putting them in her mouth to nurse on when sleep was slow in coming. She awoke one continuum and found that the light in her dungeon had turned oceanic, and she thought that the Elders might have taken offense to the natural color of moonlight and gone and bathed the helpless satellite in blue gel. She stood and caught sight of her own nebulous reflection in the dirt. What was not available to the eye, her other eye filled in, though she was working in caricature, purposely exaggerating the two protruding coral scaffoldings that formed her ribcage and the outsized scallop shell that was her new pelvis. Standing there, she had the sensation that she was actually too brittle to walk and that perhaps it might be better to lie down. She tranced upon the pipework shadow for time unmeasured before she remembered that she was an artist and started to nose around for something that would serve as a paintbrush.

She etched in the dirt, using the handle of one of the brushes De Ville had left behind—at this point, she could not recall the reason for the additional sentence, but she did have an inkling that it had something to do with the Song of Solomon. Her memory had been fictive even before she suffered persecution, and it was no stretch for her to fabricate the memory of herself reciting the Song atop the chromed Range Rover that commemorated the Mother of All Drive-bys in Honeyman Square. Her decision to decorate the floor of her cell with images from the Song's narrative was instinctual and spiteless. Years ago, she learned the bold strokes of dissent in the pamphlet illustrations of Mustapha the Apostate and in the outlaw graffiti of Il Mano Negri. She thought of the flagellants who had entered the city before the coming of Blight and who had publicly digested the underpants of their enemies to further the cause of the angels—underground, her allegiances were to a world above.

Upon that first night, or it may well have been a noontide or a waning dusk for all she knew, she took great pains in sketching the chariot and horses of King Solomon, the chariot done in outsized tondo. Knowing that the Song had it made of timber from the cedars of Lebanon, she imagined the wood to be blue with longevity, and she buffed at the dirt with a gauze-scrub until her chariot was suitably azure. When she finished, it appeared almost as if the king's flame tails were hauling the globe of the primeval earth. She drew doves in stone clefts, little foxes amid corded vines, and the rose of Sharon, though she had never seen such a flower and hers came out looking like the head of an artichoke with serrated leaves. Then, joyously misinterpreting, she drew rows of breasts with identical fawn faces stamped over the aureoles and vast ocular chambers with stenciled black bull's-eyes for pupils. When she could remember no more of the song, she riffed directly from her own imagination. She drew the bedsheet of the Queen of Sheba on the morning following the night she had come to Solomon's inner rooms to "prove him with hard questions," allowing the sheet to be stained with a rectangular Valentine, not feeling herself worthy to impugn the honor of one so inquisitive. Luckily, there was no need for her to open her veins in order to color the ancient love memento; her gums had started bleeding in the second year of her captivity and she was certain they would not be stanched until the hour of her release.

———

Over the course of the final two years of her sentence extension, she worked on the sunken bath of the late period Solomon, where he spent his days measuring the nautical strength of his own rasping breath against the still surface of the water. She dug the gulf with talons stunted after a growth of four inches. She was finished landscaping the tub and she was scratching Kama-sutra figurines into the basin when she heard the steel wings above her begin to part. She did not look up, but the sun itched in her eyes just the same.

Someone said, "Ho, shit! For a minute, I thought we opened up on Tut."

It took her several moments to access the voice—only when she was certain did she dart her eye. It was Donald Thirty-Eight F. X. Elder who had spoken. He'd ditched his golden robes in favor of a gray-trimmed black running suit with the logo of a flame running in a diagonal pattern across the breast, and had split the top of De Ville's stovepipe sable hat, wearing it like a muff along the length of his forearm. She did not recognize the Elders who were with him, although the Norwegians were fa-miliar and they looked all the more gladiatorial for the steel that had crept into their hair.

"I seen somethin' like that back in the war," Donald said, look-ing down. "Dominic Disadattato hid out with Iron Mike Cardinal O'Boyle because he thought we wouldn't fuck with no basilica. Shit, we let go with our Roman candles and I even had that nigga from the Bar Kays blowin' trumpet 'bout like Joshuway. Marble ceilin' came down and cracks run through it, but it never did bust, so I had my boys flip it back on its A-side and I walked it like ice. All them painted saints with their hands reachin' out at my boots. Tell ya, it was like God Himself stepped back and said, 'C'mon with it.' So, how you been?"

"Where's De Ville?" Electra asked.

"Cemetery. 'Bout six years ago we had this East Coast-West

Coast confusion. Rivals went and sent De Ville a concubine with a hepatotoxic clam, rest his and her souls. See, that's sorta what I wanted to talk to you about."

"No opinion."

"Truly, I did not expect one. 'Lectra, before De Ville passed, word got out through the snitches that we had you locked up down there 'cuz y'all had the buh-alls to paint that white lady in fulfillment of your reentry exam."

"What white lady?"

She forgot and looked directly up at him. The sunlight rinsed her skull with ammonia and a phosphorescent neon with a bright red checkerboard pattern blazed in the air between him and her.

"You all right, maestra? You want a night mask, or a wet towel, or somethin'?"

"What white lady?" she said, blinking.

"The white lady. The one who gave birth to whirlwind and that's how come we got sugar-frosted icing at the top of the world, or whatever it was. You know, even though we never did actually let you paint that thing, on the strength of rumor alone, I cannot give a speech, nor hand out a meritorious noose of gold without some knucklehead hoists that bitch on a banner."

"Huh?"

This time the sunlight entered her throat as her jaw came unstrung—she had the simultaneous memories of butterscotch and of the illicit hookah pipe of her days at the Academy.

"It's true," Donald insisted. "And every night, some Johnny Red Reb comes with chalk and draws her on the side of my villa. The Guard ain't spry enough to catch him, neither. I calls him 'Quick Draw.'"

His laughter was so much more genuine than De Ville's and, being real, it failed to hide his terror. She realized that he was coming to her with a matter that involved the keeping of his head upon his neck.

"See I like to keep my plebeians happy. This year, I'm gonna bring back touch-tone bingo, reintroduce testosterone back into the tap water, and I mean to unveil your white lady on a satellite hookup live from Blight's tomb on the anniversary of his assassination."

"Okay, stop," said Electra. "What my white lady got to do with G. God Blight and his moulderin' ol' body?"

"Well, most everything you do got to do with poor ol' Blight. It's strange bedfellows, I grant you, but that's the nature of the game."

"I never fellowed Blight."

"Be that as it may, somebody necktied that nigga and it was just you, him, and the good Lord in the bedroom that night."

"Say what?"

"Look, 'Lectra, I didn't come here to pick scabs and, whatever else, this here is a matter of some national urgency. Deal is this: you wet us up that white lady and I will make some calls to neutral countries. Let's see, I brung your espresso and what's that puh-jammy you liked? Let me see what's in the archives."

He reached into a Norwegian's fanny pack and pulled out a Rolodex. He fanned the file like playing cards and this seemed to cue the hydraulic crane; it hovered above, looking down its Mesozoic neck at her, then lowering the canvas on the spear-shaped spike as lightly as a lizard disdaining to swallow a fly.

"I ain't exactly got Avalon and the Average," Donald said. "How about Grande Rebbe Schlomo Weissberg live at the Copa?"

She forsook music altogether and slotted the new brushes between each of the fingers of her right hand, but in a heartbeat her hand became electrified and the brushes fell, in a jackstraw pattern, to the ground. She glanced at Donald, his smile trembling, a man neither exceptionally gallant, good, nor base—she had the very last thing she needed at that moment: a tormentor of ordinary ilk. She placed her right hand upon the center of the canvas; the heavy cloth was warm and her fingertips were half-moons in grimy eclipse, the hand pulsing counter to the will of motor function, the spasms reminding her of a spider's calibrated walk. She'd learned, in confinement, to cut her mind dead on command; it was a reflex good for getting her through the faithless nights. It was only on this particular occasion that it turned out to be a dreadful mistake—the vision was already primed upon the reef of her brain and it was allowed to skate through uncontested, a black-tipped tarantula crawling along the folds of a wedding gown. She sighed and went to sleep on her feet. Something soft and scratchy opened her eye pouch for her; for a moment, she experienced the pleasant sensation of looking at the world through a fetal mask while Donald reeled in his pool cue—it actually collapsed like a tape measure—and he put it back in his pocket.

"See, girl, much as I'd like to be lenient, everybody thinks we got us a white lady and therefore we pretty much got to have us a white lady."

"Get somebody else to paint it," she said.

"Don't you think I thought of that? What I say to the connoisseurous-rexs when they cry 'pose'?"

"Shoot them," she said.

"All of them?"

"Look, okay? I'm tired and I wasn't expecting company."

He inched forward and curled his toes around the edge of the precipice. A fine, dark mist trailed down. "Puh-leeze," he said.

"I can't."

"What do you mean? You don't remember the white lady?"

"Sure, I recollect her. You know, ice got a scent to it that's kindly hard to forget?"

"I didn't know that a'tall," Donald said.

"Surely," she said. "It's a hybrid of sick bed linen and platonic love. Do you know when it stinks the most?"

"When?" he mouthed, wordlessly.

"When it's melting. I sure do remember the white lady; I'm even startin' to smell like her."

He surprised her by turning without another word. The following morning, the entire decade's worth of work upon the dungeon had been thrashed away and so perhaps she did not merely dream the rope-haired and white-smocked children with the abortive smiles and the toy rakes, after all. She remembered asking them who they were and they beamed, ever so briefly, and answered, "Room service." She lay with one hand behind her head as a carpet of tarp was rolled across the top of the grate and the breath holes darkened with such a finality that she imagined hearing martial boots above, although there was no such sound. She had woken just prior to this visitation of darkness and she immediately rolled over onto her belly and slept for several years.

---

There was a recurrent dream of seeing a mouth in the darkness, a mouth wearing white lipstick, quivering, wide as the spout of an alpine horn, speaking only to inquire of her name and to mispronounce it after she'd said it. "Allegra?" "Elegia?" Though she was sleeping, she knew that she had been blessed with the erasure of her waking identity. Then one day the mouth bid her farewell—it kissed the air and turned to a powdery smoke, replaced by the great orb of a silver basin suspended in the pitch-black above her head. She climbed up on the air and peered into its belly. There, deep in the bowl, were shiny kernels of birdseed, bitter upon her tongue and armor-hard in the grip of her teeth. She swallowed them whole, one after the other, and felt them painting her esophagus as they dissolved. She went to sleep and awoke in a new decade with an oddly painless indigestion and the smell of roses upon her breath. Her hair had gone blonde at the roots; she knew this by the peroxide-like sizzle deep in her scalp. She lay on her back and let her hands wander in divergent paths from the top of her head to the long knives of her toes. She was five inches taller and gone was the baby fat in her hips and thighs, her buttocks had flattened into the single footprint of a camel, and the feel of her newly hardened and realigned cheekbones startled her. She found that she could wrap her palm around the handlebar of her chin.

She wanted to draw a self-portrait, but to use the stick end of one of the paintbrushes, or even her own fingerblade, seemed like poor sportsmanship at this point, so she drew her new form in the dirt, using only her pubic bone. To accomplish this, she walked on her hands and gyrated like a drunken snake, afterward reading the portrait with her fingers, and deciding that her mouth was really much fuller and her cheekbones more hawk-like than the ones drawn in the dirt. She revised until an hour she presumed was dawn, finally falling asleep, curled into a loop at the mouth of her portrait.

When it came time to do a memorial bust of De Ville, she used her clenched kneecap for the broader outline and did the finer detail with her nose and tongue. She read it like Braille and then forgot about De Ville; no, instead, the drawing was the head of an ox and it was a talisman against famine. It dawned on her that she hadn't had anything to eat for many years and she was disappointed that this should be so painless; losing her appetite seemed a sign of aging, and she found herself hungry for starvation.

When inspiration flagged, she contented herself with refurbishing the alphabet. For instance, the letter *A* took on the pronunciation "awe" and a dropsical eyeball represented it, and *B* became "buhwa," and it was pictured as a clenched fist with several extra knuckles. She sketched a personal Rosetta Stone, committed it to memory, and then rubbed it away. She embroidered the periphery of her dungeon with emblematic variations on each individual member of the alphabet. Having finished this, she used the new language to copy out what she could remember of the Song of Songs across the main living area. What she could not collect from memory, she merely padded with lyrics from Gawt Shawt and Avalon. She signed the rubricated mural with her right palm print, and moved permanently to the tiny area near the left corner of her cell, so as never to muss the work. Her revenge was minutely detailed in her mind by now. Municipal Power would one day have to excavate and the drill crew would find a skeleton sitting in lotus next to an unfathomable hiero-glyphic riot; the mad dogs of media would let loose with speculation concerning a warning of impending doom from a distant age, and the entire populace of the twenty-ninth or thirtieth century would hear the echo of Electra laughing last at them.

They came far too early for that; she heard their songoma drums, feral and close, and she decided that the drums heralded death— that it was no less than the sound of a ghost herd of prancing stallions in lieu of the sweet and low-slung chariot she had her heart set upon. She watched as the tarp above shriveled to an unruly black patch and she saw the iron wings go up, the kliegs of a thousand camera crews blazing so fiercely against the night sky that she assumed they were opening her cell so that she might witness her very first meteor shower. Her body was camouflaged in metallic grime—she rhymed so well with the color of the dirt beneath her that the spotlights scrambled and engaged in aerial dogfights in order to locate her. She heard the "oohs" and the "awws" of the crowd above and she deigned to sit upright. The searchlights merged into one single concentric circle, framing her face into an oval portrait. The crowd then parted and a boy of perhaps twelve stepped to the precipice, his shadow hanging elongated and comic along the dungeon wall. He wore a coarse Bantu tunic and his skull was clean-shaven and sphered into a perfect egg. His skin color showed not a trace of ancestral rape; his sleepy eyes held in them the jaundice of dawn. With her eyesight well preserved by a generation of darkness, she ascertained that he must be the loveless product of genetic breeding, that his parents might very well have met only in a petri dish, and her aging heart ached for him.

The boy said that he was the Ataraxia, the fifth in a line of such Ataraxias. He had no more than said it when he was obliged to step back from the microphone because his reedy voice was lariating into echo whispers and this spooked him into following the sound reverbs across the heavens, as though he expected to find his own face in the sky. She saw him gesture at what must have been a sound technician somewhere off in the distance, and she heard the screech of their fiddlings with the soundboard— the hum of a buried cathedral organ filled her ears. She looked away and then looked back to see the Ataraxia smiling down, self-consciously. There was, finally, silence and the boy spoke again. He told her how "Donald the Usurper" had hid her whereabouts in an electronic vault shortly before his execution. A team of numerologists, he said, spent many years trying in vain to crack Donald's computer code. During that time, Congress enacted legislation that named one international airport, three separate apparel outlets, one comet, and the twenty-seventh of September after her. Only the previous week, they went as far as to solicit the help of N. Finite, the numerologist who had darkened Atlantic City into a state of abject poverty two decades ago—he suggested that the numerologists throw knives at a large Bible and then play straight combinations of the wounded verse numbers. They threw their hands in the air and did as he said.

The Ataraxia called for a songoma roll; he crooked his finger in the air as the drums awakened something in her loins, which immediately rolled over and pleaded fatigue. A canvas draped in calico that reminded her of grits-house tablecloth was raised upon a flagpole, and trumpets flourished. The calico was stripped away and she saw a pale constructivist figure poised against an ashen background. The figure had a shingled face and bottomless eyes; she recognized in it the tutored hand of an academician, who had probably executed the painting while the bore of a Norwegian's shooter creased his ear and strengthened his resolve. She saw absolutely nothing of her ice woman in it and she quickly cast her eyes to the earth. It sickened her to have them think that she was only humbled by their applause, so she forced herself to look up, and she saw that many of them were weeping. The Ataraxia asked if he might interject a personal note. She said nothing, so he went ahead and told her how pleased he was to be meeting her at last and how it dulcified his soul to know that she would live on in his kingdom after he had passed.

"What makes you so sure of that?" she asked. "I 'spect you been dancin' all over my grave here since the day you learned to toddle."

"Oh, pardon me," he said, "you don't know, do you? My term expires at the third hour tonight. The sixth Ataraxia is having his head shaved right now and I am to be strangled with a pillow slip at the fourth bell."

"Why a pillow slip?" she said, certain that the boy was only goofing on her. "Fools won't allow your mother the dignity of dippin' around in your bullet holes?"

"Not at all," he answered, unfazed. "But the story has come down to us that you strangled Delroy Cooper with a pillowcase when he attempted to, pardon me, force you. In keeping with this tradition—"

"Ho, who's Delroy Cooper? Think I'd choke a muthafuckah without askin' his name?"

"Delroy Cooper is the given name of the tyrant G. God Blight, alias the Honeyman," he said. "And happy am I to die with my integrity untempted."

Upon hearing this, Electra sat down in the deep swing seat of the letter *U,* furrowed in the dirt in years long past. A brass band mangled a melody from her girlhood and a group of Yoruban dancers high-stepped across a narrow plank slung directly over her head. There was a fireworks presentation and then a barrel-sized wicker basket was lowered on wires. She would not budge from her *U.*

"But it's time for the parade," the Ataraxia said. "We got delegations from forty nations and the ice cream's already startin' to look like brain matter."

She didn't answer. He wiped his forehead and lowered his voice to a whisper.

"Auntie, what am I gonna tell them?"

"Tell them I'm tired."

"They'll just say they're tired too."

"Then tell them I'm painting."

She closed her eyes and tightened into a fetal wedge in the lap of the *U.* In the morning, they had all gone home.

**Death and the Maid**   She and Clayton and Our Boy Bubba
had eaten dinner, the dishes were done, and it was just after eight
when Sophia left the house. When she stepped down off of the
pine porch, there was only the red earth and its spitefulness
nettled the bottoms of her bare feet; the screen door, its six-inch
tear advantageous to all but the barn bats, screeched on its
hinges three times over. The footpath to the field had the worn
sheen of an old saddle and the sky was sunless, but still pale. She
guessed that she had perhaps fifteen minutes of what would
serve her better than actual daylight to say her piece in.

She was rehearsing the opening words in her head: "Well,
Mrs. Buxton . . . So, Mrs. Buxton . . . How do you do,
Mrs. Buxton?" She reached the field before she had made up her

mind. The redness of the freshly turned earth threw her. She said simply, "God," and her forearms ceased walking the air like rudimentary batons.

"Mrs. Buxton," she said, "you're not in Brownsville no more. You're in McAllen. My name is Sophia and this here's my field. I'm gonna . . . well, I'm gonna . . ."

She couldn't decide between "keep you" or "look after you" and soon she found that the choice itself dried away on her tongue. She had to lick the roof of her mouth and she tasted railing as she began to speak again. She apologized for taking up the better part of the day in getting Mrs. Buxton "settled in" and particularly for the three-hour wait in the tractor shed—her pastor was undergoing therapy for his pedophilia and she was foolish enough to put her faith in Owlington County's Reverend Heisler. When he hadn't presented himself at noon, as arranged days ago, she phoned his parsonage and spoke to a talcum-voiced female who insisted that she was his housekeeper. The housekeeper explained, with regrets, that the Reverend had sudden business in Tijuana that morning.

Sophia thought that "sudden business in Tijuana" meant he was selling his last rite writs door-to-door, or under a rock to under another rock—that is, if the city remained anything like it was on her distant and dismal honeymoon. The writs contained a Latin excerpt on the front and an adhesive patch on the back and they were commonly glued to a dying person's chest like a candy store tattoo. Sophia said that they were considered a great convenience all across the vast backyard of Texas because they saved the bereaved the trouble of summoning a clergyman at the hour of death. She wasn't even sure that the Reverend's faith—Protestant something—sanctioned extreme unction. Mrs. Buxton didn't seem to know either.

The powder-voiced housekeeper asked Sophia if she were speaking on a cell phone. Sophia told her she wasn't. The housekeeper thought that that was a pity, since she had half a mind to dial up the Reverend's hotel in Tijuana and ask that he bequeath Mrs. Buxton's "otherworldly remains" unto the Lord Almighty from the other side of the border, while Sophia held the cell phone, the one she did not happen to have, over the grave. She heard the very beginning of a hum coming from far down the gravel road that fronted the absentee-owned portion of the acreage; a speck appeared on the horizon, soon revealing itself to be a neutral-colored sedan with its headlights already on. Even with the day holding, she could not ascertain the make of the car and this unsettled her because the traffic on that road was usually limited to her neighbors. She did know that if a stranger had strayed onto her road from the interstate, then that stranger was either pitifully nearsighted or someone who had gotten lost on purpose. She held up her hand in commiseration. Across the field, the car came abreast and Sophia had to drop her hand for fear of being mistaken for a scarecrow.

"So how you like the country?" she asked, knowing that Mrs. Buxton had spent most of her life in New Jersey. She joked that Texas had much to see and most of it was hardly worth looking at—it was the size of the state and the relative paucity of human beings that pleased Sophia: "Good for keepin' things in the family, if you follow me." She talked of the free fall of crop prices over the years and how at present the average South Texas farm could not feed a family of gerbils. She told the grave how the land developers had appeared "thick as bonebirds" in the early 1980s and how much of what was once their land had been auctioned off and bonded to tract housing.

"Mexicans," she said, "dew-eyed and damp-back Mexicans and they're comin' this way. Hang around the streets of town ten minutes and you find out that they don't know the difference between a marble birdbath and public pisser. You know what I think, Mrs. Buxton? I think we're about to end up just like the Alamo."

The burial field was now all that was left of the land her husband had inherited from his father and his father from his. She and Clayton and Our Boy Bubba planted without a harvest; they sowed and they did not reap. The county gave them three hundred dollars a grave, less the occasional kickback. Weekday afternoons, she earned extra cash by delivering foil-wrapped meals from the parsonage to the elderly in the trailer towns that ringed the city limits while Bubba sometimes landscaped by day and outlawed most every night, running the interstate with a band of boys who could strip a hobbled vehicle down to its skeletal essence in a matter of minutes, and Clayton chased the roseate genie through endless jugs of border wine, and Sophia claimed to be grateful to the liquor for the tranquility it brought her husband. She sipped a glass now and then, but it tasted like "hot and sour Hi C."

"We actually manage quite well," she said.

---

She heard the screen door, loose on its hinges, and she looked back toward the house. It was only the wind. She peered as best she could from the distance, and she caught the blue phosphorescence of the television set beaming through the front window.

"'Scuze me, Mrs. Buxton," she said, "I thought that might be Clayton or Bubba come to fetch me in. Truth to tell—and I am one straight-shooter from the old school—neither one of them thought that it was necessary for me to come out and speak with you this evening. Truth is, if you'll pardon me for sayin' so, they didn't want to take you in altogether. They said you'd bring bad luck. Can you imagine? Like blamin' the rain on the sky."

She paused and waited as she would with the living. Mrs. Buxton's silence emboldened her to continue.

"Pardon me again for sayin' so, but they were rightfully suspicious, I reckon. 'Least from their standpoint. We never had a case like yours. County's sent us their vagrants and their mole peoples enough to stack like lumber. We've even had convicts. But you, ma'am, are our very first Texas State executed."

The paleness of the sky hadn't altered—the enfeebled day was squatting and listening and Sophia wished for twilight. For one thing, the burial mound seemed so obscenely red, and this reminded her of the ghastly Halloween pranks she had seen perpetrated upon defenseless graves, which were, in the end, anything but defenseless, since these acts of malice shamed only the living. Death, in all of its belligerent inevitability, was never mocked.

"But finally," she said, "I lined 'em by eye, Clayton and Bubba, and I told 'em, 'Bad luck, hell. Ain't Our Girl Aubrey a Carmelite nun-trainee with the sisters in the city of San Antonio? Why, that's just like havin' a little lobbyist up at the gates of heaven.'"

Her daughter Aubrey had seen a fanning angel in the very same field they were now conversing in. Sophia told Mrs. Buxton how the child could not be dissuaded with talk of sundown shadows and how she would neither sleep nor eat until her mother phoned the Archdiocese to report the news of the Catholic miracle. The good sisters of San Antonio had sent their van for Aubrey within the week.

"I don't miss her much on account of I know she's with God," Sophia said.

She apologized for going on about her family matters when it was really her task tonight to welcome Mrs. Buxton to the field. She explained that she felt a keen sense of duty to get to know her "interreds" as though they were relatives.

"Lost relatives, I guess you'd say," she said. "Long lost. Don't you go thinkin' I'm crazy, now. I am a Christian and a Christian believes, by book, that the dead retain an awareness of their earthly remains. It's like when I donate a blouse to Goodwill. A little while down the road I'm sure to see it in a Mex clothing stall, or maybe just some Mex kid raggin' shoes with it."

Her eyes roamed the field. "You know," she said, "maybe I better just watch what I say. This bein' the border, not everybody in this field is altogether Anglo-American."

---

"Well I ain't to judge. Likely you can't help it how you're born and I'm beginning to wonder if you can help it how you live. And although I am not to pass judgment, I am meant to try to understand within the confines of what God meant for me to learn. I said the same long before my only daughter was deemed holy and havin' one saint-child to my name has only strengthened my belief. Understanding is dearer than judgment and harder to come by, to boot. I tell you, most of the time what I understand for certain is a mystery to me. This life will knot your head like a nigger bonnet."

She paused and waited.

"Sorry."

She puffed her cheeks and let the air out, slowly. "Fact of the matter, Mrs. Buxton," she said, "the county, by law, has to inform me of the backgrounds of every body I inter. Therefore, the reason why you're lyin' here in my field has not escaped me. I asked right off about your daughter, little Muhibbi. Clerk said your mama, her grandma, had buried her up in New Jersey eight long years ago. I naturally asked why she wouldn't do the same for you, now that your debt is done and you ain't able to harm nobody else. The clerk told me he didn't know why she wouldn't have anything to do with disposing of you, but neither our county nor Texas State has any legal means with which to compel her. That's what he said and I said that's a shame. A damn sight of a shame you and your daughter ain't layin' together back where you belong. The two of you could have made it all up over eternity."

All at once the sun dimmed and Sophia saw that she was casting her shadow directly upon the grave. For fear of being thought rude, she moved slightly to her left and the shadow did not move with her. She switched back to her original position like someone trying to outwit a mirror.

"If only you hadn't done it in Texas, ma'am. I expect up in New Jersey this sorta thing happens all the time. I ain't never been there, but from what I get from the TV its pretty much one big rumpus room, ain't it? A New Jersey jury, even if they didn't believe your story, mighta stifled their shock long enough to see their way clear to send you off to an asylum. Be the most humane thing to do, if you ask me. For all goings on around here, we still don't get much daughter killin' per se. We don't have the first notion of what to do about such a thing 'cept to kill the one who done it."

She moved again and her shadow did not move; she raised her

hand and the shadow refused to wave back at her. She bit at the web of her palm and it hurt—she was alive, but dreaming; it was important for her to listen closely to what she herself had to say.

"I just got to hand it to you for sheer gumption."

She moved a step closer.

"You plain old went to bat baldface in that courtroom. Tellin' 'em all about those Nazi skinheads runnin' your car off the road. How they molested you and your daughter for three straight days and then knocked you out with a shot of dope. You woke up short a child and you drove clean across the state, huntin' for her. You never bothered to contact the police 'cuz with their big bellies and their fat, red necks, they didn't look all that much removed from the skinheads. And, right hand to God, you had no idea that your daughter was in your back trunk all the while. Neither did those eight thousand witnesses within five city blocks when you pulled into that Phillips station. They just figured maybe you had a rotted hog in the car with you."

---

She turned her back to the grave; she hunched forward and the long nozzle of her spinal column showed clearly through the fabric of her sweater, her fists balled into the base of her stomach, and her elbows in the air. Viewed from Mrs. Buxton's perspective, it would have looked as though Sophia were straining to take flight.

"I'm sorry, Mrs. Buxton," she said, turning back. "I forgot my manners. I tend to do that with my dead."

She was standing now on the roof of the grave and the earth was warmer and kinder to her toes than the outlying dirt had been. When she turned away to laugh, she had felt a breeze upon the back of her neck, and she wondered if the occupant of the grave wasn't laughing with her. Just to be certain that there was no ill will in the air, she reached down to give the earth a reassuring and apologetic pat.

"Wasn't anything personal, I hope you know," she said.

A bracelet of ice seized her wrist and her right arm wrenched forward—she found herself offering the grave the emptiness of her right hand. Again, she apologized, saying that her rudeness might have to do with something she ate and she tried, with difficulty, to recall her dinner of roughly forty-five minutes ago. The numbness of her fingertips promised an end to the needlepoint that had salvaged so many evenings for her. She gauged the tensile strength of the grip, tug of warring for an instant. Her shoulder socket began to give ground and she had to ease off.

"Mrs. Buxton, I know mothers and daughters," she said, evenly. "I've been on both sides of the issue. It's a beautiful thing, sure. Sometimes too beautiful. Havin' somebody so close to you wearin' your eyes and your former mind. Every moment and every memory comes shootin' right back at you. It's like havin' a person in your skin with ya."

She paused and waited, as she would with the living.

"I can truly say I almost understand, and understanding, honey, is a duty to me, whereas judgment abides by God. What with you bein' chased out of New Jersey by that gun-totin', cuckolded boyfriend. You wheelin' all across the country, lookin' for what work you could find on a sixth-grade certificate. Just what was you supposed to say when the child asked you, "'Where we goin' to, Mommy?'"

She felt the grip loosen a notch and she considered trying to snatch her hand free, but decided that it would be foolhardy to try to outquick the dead; the ghost would have to be lulled into letting go.

"Between you and me, we can call this thing you did self-abuse. You killed this precious little part of yourself and then you tried to keep on drivin'."

The ghost released her hand. She wanted to stand up, but, given the situation, she distrusted sudden movement. She looked back at the house; it seemed impossibly distant and remote, as though the household already slept and the house now existed only in the compression of sleep and dreams. She lived in that house for over half her lifetime. She had sex and babies and fits all within its walls. The idea that it had been a drowsy mirage

Ice Age

all along delighted her. She looked at the grave and her smile dried up.

She said to the dirt, "You tried to keep on drivin', but now you're lookin' at a red light you know damn well you can't never run."

She felt the front of her sweater separate from her skin. She murmured, "I just meant . . ." before the burning of the fabric into the back of her neck caused her jaw to clench. She was on her knees and the weight of her body upset the burial mound. The earth under her knees became larval.

"Is it that you want me to pray with you, Mrs. Buxton?" she asked, her voice going high and small. "You could have tried as-kin' kindly, you know? I never been one to shrink from prayer. I do have to have both hands, however."

The ghost did not respond and Sophia made an attempt to sound stern and severe. "Look here, do you want the good Lord to hear us or don't ya? I expect we've both given Him enough reason not to listen as it is."

Four bone-cold digits latticed into the spaces between each of the fingers of her right hand. She felt the chill down to her toes and she was afraid that she might commit the sacrilege of void-ing her bladder right where she knelt. She joined her left hand to the prayer pyramid, and though her mind was blank with ter-ror, her appeal to heaven came out as assured as a sermon.

"Dear Lord, I ask upon the soul of my daughter Aubrey, now a Carmelite nun-trainee, and upon the soul of the lost lamb Mu-hibbi, only daughter of Mrs. Yasmina Buxton, that You bestow Your grace and tender mercies upon the wayward spirit of the newly departed here with me. She is, as I am and as I have men-tioned, a mother. A chosen vessel of Your life-givin' power. You did see fit to entrust a life to her. Lord, she nurtured that child just as long as she possibly could. When she could no longer nurture and when she knew that she had no life worth givin' life to . . . well, Lord, she slaughtered."

Sophia could scarcely believe that she had said that, nor could she believe that she was presently being pulled face-first into the burial dirt with her arm contorting higher and higher up her back. She opened her mouth to protest and she tasted earth. She felt her fingers bending back toward the joints and she saw a succession of blue-steel match heads, flaring into tiny zips of lightning.

"She slaughtered in the spirit of sacrifice," she got out between clenched teeth. "In accord with Abraham and Isaac and all that. Believin' that it was to Your will and Your greater glory and that she was only givin' You back what was Yours all along."

---

Her arm fell freely down her back, as limp as a sleeper's. She had bitten into her tongue and when she spat the issue was darker for the combination of blood and earth. She remembered that it was a grave she was lying upon and she said, "Sorry, ma'am." She wiped the spot with her fingertips and patted at the earth.

"That's all right," she said, nursing her bitten tongue. "I ain't about to get into a fight with someone on their first full day of bein' dead. I would like you to know that your quarrel is not with me. I mean, I've lost just like you. It wasn't that awful long ago I had fifteen hundred whole acres of land and a daughter closer to me than my own heartbeat."

She pushed herself up by her elbows; she stood there, shaking the dirt from her hair. She smiled down at the grave through the cloud of fine gravel she had just filled the air with, her own blood now bright at the corner of her lip.

"Do you know what my heart whispers to me, Mrs. Buxton? It whispers, 'Good for you.' Night and day, that's all I hear from my heart. 'Good for you, good for you, good for you.' Well, all right, good for me. 'Cuz I let my lamb bleed, lady, and you best believe you never did. You just hung on to your girl's windpipe for three minutes and she had heaven on a plate. Aubrey, hell, she ain't in no convent. That's just somethin' I tell in town when they ask me where my youngest is at. One too many times I had to chase her off from over yonder, our sold-off fields. I says to her, 'Girl, you mean to tell me I sent you to school for five-and-a-half whole grades and you can't so much as read "no trespassing?" It ain't like you ever worked this land or lost any sleep worryin' about an early frost, or the grasshoppers, or the blood mortgages on it? This here's my field, or least it was. Maybe it's time for you to find your own land. Get somethin' of your own and then lose it, so you'll know what I know. County workers are always sayin' how thin and peaked you look; I got me a mind to let them take you off my hands.'"

She waited as she would with the living.

"Then the county came, Mrs. Buxton. Aubrey didn't wanna get in the car with them. My eyes stayed dry. I just said, 'Go on, Lamb. Go on up the road. Go on and bleed like I bleed.'"

———

The north wind struck her full in the face; it electrified her clothes and she felt bits of Mrs. Buxton's soil spraying her ankles. She looked around and saw that night had fallen.

"There ain't hardly a man, woman, child in the county doesn't know what I did," she said. "But I'll be goddamned if I'll ever admit it to a livin' soul. So, much obliged, Mrs. Buxton. I'm gonna have to get back to the house now; it's past time I be on about my business. Might be I'll be back to check on you, I don't know. Depends on how heavy Clayton and Bubba sleep tonight. Mind you don't move around too much and disturb the other residents. You try to get some rest now, y'hear?"

She turned up the path. She halted, digging in her heels. She said, "Oh, the rock," and she hurried back to the grave.

"Mrs. Buxton, I usually take a small rock from the grave of a new arrival. I like to wear it in my apron for a day or two and then I put it in the breakfront in the dining room with the others. It's a memento of the bond between me and my inter-reds. May I?"

She reached down and the icy bracelet again closed around her wrist—she did not struggle.

"Mrs. Buxton," she said, "would you like to come in the house?"

**Photographs: Rub Al Khali, 1990–91**   The field hospital I was stationed in was nicknamed "Iceland." It was always chilly in the wards; there was frosted glass everywhere. The hospital wasn't housed in a burlap tent like in the movies; it was built of quick, corrugated iron and there was a separate generator for the air-conditioning unit alone, a hunchbacked green dynamo that sweated cold in the desert sun. We called it "Erwin Rommel." A lot of the medical gadgetry was unfamiliar, but incredibly light-weight, ingenious, and indispensable, and I assume that these devices were held back from the civilian market for the same reason pike-axes were not commonly sold along the roadside in the fourteenth century—some things must be reserved for the eventuality of war.

The real war was the waiting; the personnel drills were the dream. Lime-green space music and battle soundtracks played in the O.R.; you heard fuse whispers, cannonade, machine-gun stutters. The vapor of ammonia lodged in your nose and throat. The tart smoke drifted to your brain. At night I dreamt of smoking transparencies wheeling gurneys, and bleeding mannequins, and the wind; the desert wind at night has something of the rise and fall of the sea, but nothing of the heaviness of the tide. There's the constant sound of the sky peeling, layer-by-layer, as though God were reading the night the way you would a newspaper, a newspaper dated Night One, Year One—there is no history in the desert, no evidence of any.

<hr />

There was to be no future, either. One hundred hours of actual air/land war and five hundred friendly dead. There were scores of field hospitals; no one actually died in Iceland. In memory this footnote makes the place more ghostly still. Previous to the fighting, soldiers would come in with sunstroke and eye irritations. They would look past you as you treated them, avoiding the mirrored walls as well, at the mahjong-tiled floor or at the framed prints of the Pacific surf and the Baja cliffs, which hung everywhere in innumerable variations. They looked through you with annoyance and absorption, as though you were trying to obstruct their view of their own funerals. You didn't speak of the States, or ask about their wives or their girlfriends. The topic that I remember—the ice mallet—was the rumored air caravan to Switzerland. Every other minute there was a metal tune overhead and the armored walls would hum, the glass threatening to splinter as the airplane's high note reached its threshold. I had no way of knowing if the jet was civilian or military, but always I would say, "There goes more of the neighborhood. In Riyadh they're trading their given names for cash and getting out." I would say it disparagingly, but the very idea seemed enchanting—that you could really travel that light. Then I would pass on the buzz joke, the one they'd heard a thousand times, the contagious play on the name of the country we were sent to defend: "Ku-wait, just Ku-wait."

———————

Before the bombing, there was leave, R 'n R, though if you were a woman and you went off base, you had to dress like a black mummy. Supply issued muslin gowns and guillotine hoods, felt-like, with the flesh of a poppy. When I pulled mine over my head, I would see all the burning needles it took to sew the Rub al Khali. This was the richest country in the world, armed beyond the dreams of science fiction courtesy of its Allied friends, and every bit of the topography seemed delicately hand-made, particularly the desert, the sheerest gauze lying over the bleached rocks in the sunset, the silver whips in the curl of the drifts, and the precise staining of the shadow work in the noon. One day a trafficker, seeing my white brow and gray eyes through the eyelet of my chador, held up a blanket of pink tissue paper, pink and festive in the sun. He drew out a robe of camlet, a weave of goat's hair, silk, and wool. I learned that the pattern was called "ikat" and that its uncommon blending of color and texture was achieved through weaving the warped portions of the silk, wool, and goat's coat back and forth, never allowing the blends to intersect, but rather causing them to reflect each other in a prism. It struck me that the weave paralleled the composi-tion of flames; the oxygen and kindling and the gaseous products of fire also dance without touching. Two methods, I was re-minded, friction and percussion, produce fire. In the abstract, these are also the occasions of war.

I spread the robe out on my bunk at night and read it like a prophesying diary. In the fugue of the stitching there was fire and war, but most prominent was the desert, the branded motif of shadow mirroring shadow, and the theorem of eternity with-out beginning, end, or evidence of history. I did not expect to die, however real the possibility. I simply wasn't trained to die. I rehearsed the death of others; there was even something of an oath in the ranks, way back, at the completion of the army nurs-ing training, something that mentioned the "giving of your life freely" to medicine. The understanding all along was that I was to come to know death much better than those who were to die. In the desert alone, it made sense, this giving of your life freely, here alone, where the night wind would find no dilemma in smoothing over the projectile scars in the sky and filling in the bomb craters, as well as the haphazard dead who might lie without graves. In the desert alone, my life was a gift I could afford to give without expecting anything in return.

There were craft books in the base library and a languorous clock with a hypothetical gun pointed at its head. If there had only been a looming war while I was in nurse's training. Learning to knit was just that easy. Though something was always created, the mantra of the needles was an act of deconstruction, a subterfuge like the needlework of the clock. Through the evenings I looped over all of the mental letters I'd written. Some of them were written on paper, but none of them were actually sent. I traced the white, the black tongue of revision over all of the things I had ever wished I'd said. If drilling was a way of learning to cope with death, then knitting was a way of making friends with myself. Finished, in my bunk with the lights out, with writer's cramp and a blank mind, I never felt like a healer.

There was one blanket I remember, the sewing done in a damask pattern of softly petaled wings, wide as palm leaves. Even from across the room the blanket had an ornithological luxuriance to it. The other nurses would ask to borrow it, as though I could get an inch of sleep without it. Sullen at being refused— remember they were also indoctrinated with this brain marinade of "giving freely"—they would ask if I copied the design from a book. I told them, truthfully, no, and they inevitably asked how I thought of it. But I hadn't thought of it, any more than the fabulist/geniuses, the poets and engineers, "thought" of the abstractions that they endowed with wings: the archangels and cherubs, the violin, the oboe, the missile. Anyway, the template could be seen past the enforced Plexiglas windows of the hospital. In the desert transformation and flight, the stuff of legends, are not concepts; they are reflexes. Their question annoyed me because I knew long before I came that all gods are either bred or tempted in the desert. I spent six months on the edge of the Empty Quarter, arrived and departed with the same storybook impression: that the desert is a place of sacred ablutions and winged pilgrimages—the site of the world's most ancient holding pattern. When the war was over, I left the blanket on my bunk.

---

There were walk-ins full of Demerol and Veronal and opiates with the names of obscure medieval heresiarchs. The doctors prescribed salt tablets and saline irrigations, and blamed the symptoms of the nurses—sluggishness, disconnection—on stress and the climate. Once, very late at night, I went into the latrine with a handful of smooth, emblematized beads in my hand. I don't even remember what they were. The stalls had a pale camouflage tint, an undercurrent of dysentery. I saw myself reflected in the paint job, sitting there on the toilet, looking at the tablets with a nervous, sickly smile, the acquiescence of a skull. I dripped the tablets into the bowl and watched the water turn crystalline.

---

One night we stood in ranks outside "Iceland," I in the first row, listening to the captain from the Engineering Corps. He told us that the Scuds, in their present position, would barely rattle the china in the major's quarters, but if the Iraqi army should gain ground, we might very well find ourselves working under shelling. Our mothers and grandmothers had done it in ancestral wars, and this was why we were free today. To serve in this war. He said that he had every confidence we would "stand up under fire."

There were hundreds of dogs in a kennel on the hospital grounds. They were trained to sniff out the cyanide and the bacterial compounds in the bomb canisters. The handlers roused them out of the pen with an air whistle so faint as to be a hypnotic suggestion. I listen for it still in the wind. They lined as for a race and the captain and the other officers stood in a circle to the side, chattering, joking, in raw contrast to the stolidity of the hounds. I was drilled not to let my eyes drift at attention, but I would not have been at attention at all if I hadn't been looking at the officers. Watching peripherally is like reading a story; the mind's eye participates. One of them asked for a cigarette and the captain from the Engineering Corps laughed and said, "What's that, your last request?"

His cigarette case kindled in the moonlight. He took a Zippo from his shirt pocket and rolled the flint wheel back and forth under his thumb. Then it was day—an accelerated sunrise, sounding thunder—a painted day that gave depth to the ore carpet of the Empty Quarter and to the returning blue of the heavens. There was a bronze cocoon with a burning tail up above; it hung there, roaring at gravity as the Patriot interceptor sailed by far to the right. It missed the broad side of the wasteland sky, and just for an instant there was a crimson hole at the zenith, the orb of a trapdoor opening. It was night once again and there was an echo, and two smoking columns across the sky—the smoke of an aurora having passed. We waited, still at attention as the wind brought the smoke and the sand. I closed my eyes and covered my nose and mouth. I felt the particles scratching against the fabric of my fatigues and collecting in the bill of my hat. It went cleanly through the sieve of my hand and a purified acid gathered in my sinuses. I coughed and retched, heard vomiting behind, stepped forward out of the ranks, and turned and saw so many of the others on their knees.

---

The captain from the Engineering Corps turned to us, wiping the soot from his eyes, the cap in his hand fanning. He said, "Congratulations, people, you have just seen history."

**Echo**   She has opted to die in her home in Elmira and she has not visited the neighborhood of Washington Heights in over twenty years. This is of no consequence; the passage of time and the nightly purification ritual of Newports and a bath scented with Avon Blue Hyssop is a ceremony of prayer and memory is God. Her skin is smooth, her liver is cirrhotic, and her lungs are two flasks of soot. She sits in the front room with the drapes drawn tightly. It is time. Another curtain opens.

---

"It's been ten years," her father says.

"No, dear," her mother answers, "it's been ten years since it's been ten years."

This closes the conversation for the time being.

She is in her bedroom. She loves the night, but she wishes for brightness here in her home. Her parents courted in the beer pavilions of Hell's Kitchen, where they languished after the fights or an evening of ice hockey. They moved into an uncle's apartment upon their marriage and his unsuccessful heart surgery. They unscrewed all of the overhead bulbs and purchased, from Orbachs's, a set of anemic table lamps shaded by coned pink parasols. They didn't allow her a dog or a cat, and when her mother's philodendron had been with them for three months it passed away of malnutrition. She is the only thing that has grown in this dimness.

Her mother and father have not spoken in half an hour. She now hears her father say, "So, how old's that make her?"

"Thirty-seven," her mother says.

"Mother of God."

She is waiting for them to go to bed. They work the dawning shift in the meatpacking plant that Joe Nulty sold to the Sobel Brothers just before he went to jail two years ago.

"Can't a man pity her?" her father says.

"He can pity her all day and all night and it won't put a ring on her finger or get another child from her."

"It'll get him to heaven."

"Lots of things will get him to heaven. When you were young, you didn't give a thought to marryin' for charity neither, did you?"

"What makes you so sure?" he says.

"Deirdre," her mother calls, pretending not to know. "Have you gone to sleep?"

"Yes, Mom."

The light beneath her window blinks out at nine-thirty. She has her lavender dress on and she is framed in her special window. The building dates from the nineties and it is a thing of worship in the moonlight—it is a weathered bronze with jutting, frosted edges and a vertical row of tinted glass ovalettes stitching up the northwest side, one of them intersecting her window. Standing at the glass and knowing that no one is really looking at her, she imagines seeing herself from the outside, painted upon the face of a floating diamond. She thinks of a bombed atelier or a roofless portrait gallery, naked to the night sky. She fancies herself one of the likenesses in the gallery and she holds conversation with the stars, solely in eye contact. She smiles and turns on the bedside lamp. She tiptoes from the apartment. She is going to work.

---

Stylianos's mother was hopelessly alcoholic and religious. She was a converted Jehovah's Witness who was too timid to proselytize. Instead, she raised her illegitimate son to see himself as the female reincarnation of Jesus Christ. She lathered him with patchouli, after bathing him with Avon Blue Hyssop, and taught him to sing harmony to her stupefied contralto as the two of them pestered the Almighty through the long evenings. She worked at the Botanica Santa Inez on 170th Street, and Stylianos would wait at home for her with the devotion of a house pet. Deirdre, as a child, would come out of the front door and see him on the steps, his dark hair lacquered across the back of his T-shirt like an ashen river. In the first months after they moved into their building, she would say, "Hi, ya," and get not even a glance. One day she returned from the park and, though she was sick of trying, she begrudged him one last "Hi, ya."

"Me, too," he answered.

She went upstairs and asked her mother about him.

"Is Stylianos Spanish or is he retarded?"

"Deirdre, don't be unkind."

"Well, what's a polite word for him?"

Her mother gave the question a moment of thought.

"He's deficient, sweetheart. He's a little bit deficient."

Deirdre's mother's vocabulary and indeed the whole of her adult education was informed by network quiz shows such as *The $64,000 Question*. She previously used the word "deficient" when chiding Deirdre for hurrying through her homework and her morning shower. Deirdre thought that her mother was saying that Stylianos was someone who gave short shrift to the necessary duties of life, such as studying and maintaining one's personal hygiene. She was puzzled but, as was her nature, she felt compelled to have the last word.

"He sure has clean hair for a deficient," she said. "And he smells like he lives in the tub."

---

A man from Child Welfare escorted Stylianos to the opening day of the sixth grade. His mother had apologized to a series of dark-suited visitors. She told them that she had taken it upon herself to teach him to read and to write and, in addition, she'd given him some rudimentary carpentry lessons. In her country, she let them know, children without fathers saw the inside of a school-house only in times of martial law, when the jails overflowed. A week later, Stylianos was sitting next to Deirdre in her fifth-grade geography class. Her own legs were cramped beneath her desk and the legs of the desk provided for him fairly rode the air. He was reading something called "*Arturo el Rey para Ninos*" behind the shield of his Holt and Rinehart textbook. When called upon in class, he would answer in Spanish and he spoke so rapidly that even the Nuyorican children could only guess at what he was saying. Deirdre was privately convinced that he was telling Sister Mary Magnus to break her vow of chastity with herself.

His cannon-shot eyes and his rigid, five-foot-eight-inch frame kept the other children from sporting with him for the better part of the first month. Then one afternoon in the playground she saw him entrapped in a daisy chain of light complexioned, off-blonde Irish runts. They tore the buttons from his coat with laser strikes of their grass-grimed hands and he slapped back, she thought, like a porpoise. He would or could not fight in earnest, even when he lay there on the blacktop with a bantam pair of corduroy-covered buttocks pressed against his face; neither could he cry.

She muffled the ache she felt for him behind the armor of her juvenile dignity. He couldn't have seen her, could not have been looking at her through the posterior mask he was wearing on his right cheek, and yet she could feel his eyes burning into the back of her head as she turned away from the scene. Moments later, the recess bell caused her to jump, the skipping rope she was holding as dead as a vine in her hand and a cold venom leaking into her stomach.

The Special Education program claimed him; these classes were conducted at the opposite end of the school building and she saw less and less of him. The Special Ed kids were pariahs of only a slightly higher cast than the Catholic children who attended public school—they were all but consigned to the Devil—and Stylianos seemed to be bearing his disgrace in isolation. Once, she rounded a blind corner of her apartment house's stairway with a Moviola velocity and it was all she could do to murmur, "Me, too," as he breezed by. She did happen to notice that his hair had been cut short. If he had stood still for one bare moment, she might have asked him, despite herself, if any part of his discarded mane was still available. As she climbed to the next floor, the fantasy began to take shape in her mind. It involved a string-drawn bag of velour filled with the black garden of his hair and the mist of her mother's Nightingale eau de toilette. She would go to sleep with her nose and mouth in this purse of Arabian bouquets as her asthmatic cousin did with her camphor sack.

---

In the ninth grade, Deirdre became secretly betrothed to Hughie Kearney. He played basketball well enough to have broken the arm of an opposing point guard, and he was capable of sending a flattened stone sailing and skidding for nearly half a city block. Also, he accepted as a symptom of maturity the fact that she loved the prickly feel of his brush cut against the cup of her hand—she could hardly wait for him to sprout razor stubble.

That summer Hughie and half the neighborhood were away at camp. Her parents, raised under the old Third Avenue El in the fabled Dead End District, were conditioned to look upon the outer environs as seedbeds of lethal cockroaches and as yet undiscovered species of cancer. They only possessed one daughter and they weren't going to risk her to the country, Catholic camp or no Catholic camp. This was also the summer that moonlight began to conduct chemistry experiments upon her body, totally against her will. Sleepless, she would yo-yo in the chamber of her building's elevator for hours at a time, vacillating between the eleventh floor and the lobby until near to dawn. Late one night, she chanced the structure's rooftop. The roof was as off-limits to her as the country. In their youth her parents had known a clique of well-meaning neighborhood boys who were not only without a proper playground, but also lacked something so essential as a rubber ball to toss between them. They played catch with a dead cat upon their tenement's roof. The youngest among them went out for a long one and invoked the sacred name of DiMaggio as he followed the cat over the ledge and into the sky. Deirdre was told the story so many times that not only did the prospect of the roof alarm and excite her, she was also leery of and exhilarated by the idea of falling cat corpses.

The door to the rooftop was held open by a single brick that she was sure not to disturb for fear of being marooned up there until the super came to unclog the storm drains in October. There was a glass gazebo, which she'd heard of but had never seen. The gazebo reminded her of an igloo—it was round, squat and spotted white with the scorn of bomber pigeons. There were two pieces of lawn furniture inside, both frayed and filthy, and a striped beach blanket, smoky with the olfactoric odors of its previous users. Not trusting the lawn chairs, she lay down upon the blanket, despite its noxiousness. She opened her bathrobe, although she had nothing underneath, save sweat. She would cool the cooking fat from her body and then go downstairs to bed. The sky, through the gazebo's glass, was refracted and funneled; she imagined looking up the spout of an overturned and never-ending top hat.

As a child, Deirdre would secrete ice cubes in her palms and she would marvel at how the electrified jewels would defy her greed to possess them by turning to water and escaping onto the floor. On the roof that night, she dreamt of a thin, silver cord, which she was obliged to climb. The dream cord bit into her hands and drew the veil from the tactile memory. Immediately, the cord began to melt and she slithered down the vine with cold water spraying through her hands and onto her face. Tearing and blinking, she vaguely made out Stylianos sitting there in the membranous space just above her head. He was playing the recorder. She could hear the music and she saw the extended silver pipe of the instrument, but she could not see his face because the head of dawn rested squarely between his shoulders like a burning pumpkin. She snapped the folds of her nightgown together.

"If then the father so clothe the grass," Stylianos said, "so much more shall he clothe you." He put the stem of the recorder back into his mouth.

He said it in a pitch that was unlike anything but the pleading of a cat. His voice had gotten higher as he matured since his mother, continuing her experimentation with her son's gender, had him wearing undersized satin underwear. The voice disarmed her, whereas the statement alone would have sent her running. She asked him what time it was and she learned, first, the hour, and then the news that her mother and father had alerted the police. They were scouring the parks and dragging the public swimming pools for evidence of her; the neighborhood ladies were already gathering over coffee and whittling down the list of miscreants possibly responsible for her rape and dismemberment.

Dread—the oven blast of her father's stale beer breath and her mother's averted eyes and trembling lower lip were now a certainty—always had the effect of making her sleepy. There was nothing for her to do but to roll over onto her side and listen to his recorder as it spun unseen gold. Slumber came to her again, so near and so soon, that she asked him to tell her a bedtime story in reverse, some tale to rouse her awake once more. He put the recorder in the slot between his knees and he thought for a moment. He began reciting the Gospel According to Saint Matthew virtually verbatim, beginning with the passage concerning who begot whom. She interrupted, telling him that she would rather hear the recorder after all. He put the mouthpiece to his lips and reared his head back. The sun revealed molten crystals in his sylvan hair and his jaw line held a razor sheen like that of a halo. He faltered for a short time, privately insulted, and then he hit stride with a passage of legato notes, which tumbled down on her like a warm summer rain.

---

In Elmira she feels the tarp of the night sky tightening against the oncoming storm. She turns from the television program that she has been watching solely for its redeeming blue cast and steps out of her dress. A canopy of plastic insulates the back porch; there's sufficient moonlight to paint her shadow upon the clear curtain. Moving forward she watches, in shadowplay, as the dough of her breasts and belly sags in tandem with the collapse of the sky. She is moving down the steps when the foundation rolls above and lightning clusters suddenly forge the revelation of day. There's a parasol above her birdbath. She steps beneath it with the skin of her back streaming. She dips her head and drinks, her lips creating electrified waves in the surface of the pool. She tastes the metal of the lightning and the salt of Stylianos's skin.

---

He would tell her to open her eyes. He would say to keep them open and, if she even blinked, he would bark her lids open once more. She told him that he made her feel like a dead body. He said, "You mean, I kill ya?" She pressed him and he admitted that during lovemaking he liked to watch the angel dance upon the head of a pin, the one that was rimmed by the green iris of her right pupil. But for ordering her to open her eyes, he was so silent that her own responses embarrassed her. She tried to make love like him, but, in his eyes, she looked shrunken and sad, as though a great door had shut in her face and her despondency was showing clearly in the mirrored brass knocker. The moment she liked best was when it was finished, newly finished and both of them could hardly breathe. She would imagine that their bodies were two candles, simultaneously extinguished, and that a twine of smoke, the absolute color of mortality, was knitting the air between them. The bond, she thought, was so fragile and endearing that even an ill wind would not cheapen itself by dispersing it.

———

Years later she would confide that she had become a woman and a mother all in the space of one menstrual cycle. It was very nearly true; in the few periods she had had before the advent of the pregnancy, she was troubled by the lack of cramps and lethargy. She ended up feeling like she wasn't going to make much of a woman after all. One morning she was breakfasting in the Four Brothers Four Pancake Emporium. The hotcakes arrived, steaming and fanned into a sunflower pattern. At the very edge of the plate, a single sausage bisected a clump of rubbered eggs. She got up and ran for the ladies room, as even the memory of the meal turned out the lining of her stomach. When she returned to the table, she saw that her mother had thought to cover the breakfast plate with napkins.

Her mother said, "At least tell me it's gonna be white and Catholic."

There were no explosions at home. Her father said that the pregnancy was a judgment against them all—Deirdre being too insignificant a being to have alone brought this upon them. God was testing their faith. She surprised herself by speaking up and saying that he made it sound like she had cancer rather than a fetus inside her.

Her father said, "If it were a choice between the two . . ."

Deirdre resolved to kill herself once her mood lightened.

"Do you know who it was?" her mother asked.

———

Her father consulted with Father Carney, who'd baptized, confessed, and confirmed her. The Father said he was genuinely saddened that he could do nothing to salvage her honor, but if she was brought to confession before nightfall, he would negotiate the absolution of her sin. Her father told him to never mind about all that, he was worried about the blackening of his own soul by way of murder. Father Carney proposed that they go across the street and have a drink together. It was a large drink, a full bottle in fact, and before the bottle was drained her father was on the pay phone to his two old-maid brothers, congratulating them since they were about to become great-uncles to "a little brown bastard with all of our bloods in it." They were in the tavern within minutes and the foursome made their way uptown to the Botanica.

Stylianos's mother was aghast to learn that her son had been ruined. She threatened a lawsuit if she chanced to find a single bruise upon his body. Deirdre's father happened to glance down at the display cabinet he was leaning against; he saw that it contained tiny pieces of the true cross.

"I'd like me eight dozen of these to patch the wall I put your boy's head through," he said.

Her eyes ignited. She said something in Spanish.

"And don't be thinkin' you can talk your way out of this in the devil's tongue."

Father Carney suggested that the discussion abstain from further mention of the devil. Stylianos's mother said she was willing, to the greater good, to accept a thousand dollars with which to board her son in Puerto Rico for the duration of the pregnancy.

Deirdre's Uncle Roderick said, "His whole hide's not worth one-thousand dollars. How will we give you that just for hidin' it?"

Stylianos's mother countered that her son had recently run tap water into ten mason jars and, in days, the water had fermented into wine.

"That's only the beginning of it," Deirdre's Uncle Seamus said. "Next he'll be waterin' your whiskey."

Father Carney raised the question of which party was to take charge of the newborn. In the silence, he experienced sunstroke from the looks they gave him. He turned to ask Uncle Roderick if he would be kind enough to get him a cup of water and Roderick was not where he had been a moment ago.

"Where's your older brother gone?" he asked Deirdre's father. Just then Roderick appeared in the doorway, fresh from the poultry market next door. He held in his hands a cock with a wrung neck. He laid it on top of the display case and it convulsed one last time over the fragments of the true cross.

"Have we come to an agreement?" her father said.

---

Through her glass ovalette, Deirdre watched as Stylianos got into the gypsy lorry that would take him to the airport, and she felt both the flame of her loins and the drum of her heart journeying to the pit of her swelling belly. She pitied him his thinness and bodily solitude, thinking that she had gotten the better of their exchange.

Prior to the birth, Father Carney visited her, along with a lady from Child Welfare. They both warned her not to look at the baby when it came. Father Carney offered the example of Lot's wife and he asked her if she would like to wear a surgical mask over her face. Deirdre looked around for weaponry. Her perfect houseguest of nine months had no wish to leave. He hadn't, as she'd expected, prevented her from tying her shoelaces, and he'd caused her hardly more turbulence than a second egg cream might have. But here in the closing moments of his pleasant stay, he managed to deflate her uterine wall and nearly caused her to drown in her own blood. She could not help but open her eyes to see who he was. The nameless child hung in the air, his tiny brow slowly breaking and his eyes searching for a contact point of sympathy in his three-inch span of vision. She tried to memorize his features and she focused on the pulsing birthmark that ran, like a purposeful brushstroke, from the center of his forehead to the bridge of his nose. She thought to herself that she very likely would choose it there since it set off his father's eyes. She reached her hand out. The baby contributed the memory of his scream. A nurse came and took him away.

---

It is 82 degrees at 11:09 P.M. She bids the driver to stop a street too early. She kisses a Kleenex and lets it fall to the floor, knowing that the next customer will ride in the nebula of her perfume and will undoubtedly pluck the white memento from among the flattened cigarette butts on the carpet. She steps onto a Harlem street corner where she is the only female unspoken for; her mystery alone will see her safely. She walks one full block, head on into the downtown traffic and there are no catcalls, no whistling. Instead there are only monochromatic eyes with their safeties off and the whir of window fans above her head, siphoning off what little air there is tonight.

The bartender lights her cigarette. He hands her four quarters even before she can take the bill from her purse. She splits the coins between "On Green Dolphin Street" and "Corcovado." She sips diluted champagne. The bartender keeps complimenting her on her lavender dress, saying that it pinks her skin like a warm shower. She grows tired of having to say, "Thank you," and finally tells him that she doesn't like hearing a man's dick when he is speaking with his mouth.

The first serious one tonight also admires the color of her dress. He says that he wants the same shade of lavender for the casement of his coffin. Deirdre bites her tongue in earnest. He asks her if she would like to go downtown. She says that he is mistaking her for a tourist. He forces a laugh and he is nonchalant when she mentions money, as though he has known all along. They cross the street to the old man's building. There's a brood of kids on the stoop and she smiles back at them, as she does every night. The man, not privy to their understanding, glares at the children and they alter the complexion of their smiles to a color that she does not like at all.

"They know me," she whispers to the man.

The old man does not bother to turn off his television as he starts to leave the apartment. She asks if he is wearing a watch. He peels his sleeve and shows it to her. She asks that he go no farther than the corner, because the greater the distance he covers, the more careless he is with the time that he is meant to keep for her. She secretly wishes that he could really be sent away, that the indentation of his buttocks in the sofa would smooth out, and that the smell of him in the bedding could be absorbed into the atmosphere. She takes a sheet, rolled tight as a bandage, from her purse. She unravels it and covers her side of the bed. She arranges her jewelry—two rings, a bracelet, a brooch—on the night table so that her eyes will have someplace to go.

---

The second serious one is a man legally blind and drunk, his broad tie festooned with spillage. Over and over again, she has to guide the gin glass to his lips, the feel of it cold and electric with his trembling. He is the kind who she must ask outright and she must see the money before she vacates her barstool—protocol demands that no one overhear, though those who do not know are those beyond the point of caring. She spends a worrisome amount of time waiting for the adjacent stools to be cleared. She gives up and takes him by the hand into the phone booth. Playacting, she puts the receiver to his ear and speaks directly into his eyes, her lips rounding each syllable a half inch from the rim of his smoke-colored glasses. He understands and hands her a roll of bills. She counts beneath the overhang of the phone's ledge, skimming only an extra hundred out of principle. The walk up the old man's stairs disorients the legally blind man and she is able to take a shower on his time. He calls to her from the bed. She has told him that her name is Glenda, but he keeps pronouncing it "Glinda." Later, at the oddest moment, she visualizes the Good Witch of the North.

The third client is a man who tells her that he is forty years old and has never slept with a white woman.

"Between tryin' and dyin'," he says, "just once won't hurt me."

Tonight is to be no exception for him. He apologizes in a despairing tone, telling her that his daughter has just died and that the money he has given her was to go for her funeral. Deirdre asks him what the girl died of.

"Analgesia," he says. "My baby died of analgesia."

The rest of the men and the remainder of the night are a blur. The bartender—still smarting over the suggestion that his utterances smelled of dick—stops watering her champagne, hoping that the flush of the liquor will startle her when she checks her compact and send her hurrying home to bed. A rival asks her to stop dominating the jukebox. Deirdre has it "pussywhipped," she says. She punches in "Corcovado" one last time and slow-dances with the bartender's girlfriend. The lounge lights fade and the moonlight possesses every glass vessel in the room.

---

She likes the percussion of her heels on the sidewalk and the slither of the breeze through her nylons. She must walk the three blocks to the car service because all the Yellow Cabs have migrated south hours ago. She is myopic with drink. When she first sees the boy, she thinks that he is riding an invisible broomstick three feet from the ground. It's only when she hears the lock of the wheels that she notices the bicycle beneath him. His face, below the feathered helmet of his black hair, is whited over with what looks like cold cream. Black seams are stenciled across his forehead and cheeks. He looks, to Deirdre, like someone going to a Halloween party disguised as a soccer ball.

"I'm off," she says as a reflex.

"Me, too," he answers, dipping his head in grave agreement.

There's a siren sounding in the distance, as though to remind her to be afraid. Instead, she would like to laugh and she would like him to laugh too. She wants to see if his teeth will appear yellow against the bleached background of his skin and if his tongue will glow a vivid red.

"So, aren't you going to say, 'Trick or treat?'" she says, hoping for at least a smile.

"I was hoping you would," he tells her, his voice half-submerged in shyness.

She asks him to repeat that, not because she does not understand but because she suspects that he doesn't.

He says, "You know, trick?"

She tells him that she has to see the money, knowing full well that there is none. He cracks his wallet and she sees the rim of a green-coated novella.

"Where'd you get it?"

"I didn't ask you."

"What?"

"What you have that I want."

She has no idea what he is saying, but she laughs so that his expression will change. This doesn't happen. The black stitchings tighten and his skin seems to stretch without any of the facial muscles having moved. It's a death's-head now, looking at her through the gauze of a fishing net.

"Who are you?"

"I didn't ask you."

He hurls the bicycle into the high weeds of the lot beyond the sidewalk.

---

The old man has to be coaxed to the door, and getting him to open it is a separate episode. She has the boy scrape one of his larger bills along the crack beneath the door. He says that, for the life of him, his old legs will not take him down those stairs, let alone up, once more tonight. He pulls his rocker out into the hallway without bothering to put on his pants. He promises to knock in half an hour. Deirdre closes the door and throws the dead bolt. The boy undresses in the bedroom while she searches through the old man's cupboards. He hears her and calls out, asking what she is looking for.

"Liquor," she hollers back. She is not lying and she is not telling the truth—another drink would be welcome, but what she would really like to find is the lining of this dream. She would like to tear it open and peek her head into her dawning bedroom, and then roll over onto her belly, having ventilated the hallucination with the light of day. When he calls again, she is sitting on the tile floor, seriously considering taking a drink from a bottle of grenadine. She stands and goes into the bedroom. He has laid out the money on one of the pillows, as one would cushion a gift given to a queen. He is naked now, and except for his neck and forearms he is impossibly light for a Nuyorican.

"Go draw a bath," she tells him. "You smell like an antique fish tank."

"I washed before I went out."

"Where you been since then?"

He goes into the bathroom. The tap thunders and she yells for him to close the door. She counts the money. She finds his generosity malicious—he is implicating her in whatever crimes he committed to get the money, in addition to entangling her in the unlawful act that he wishes to spend it on. The suddenness of the thought deadens her mind. The tap in the bathroom shuts off far too early. Does he intend to lie in three inches of water?

"How much time do we have left?" he calls through the wall.

Deirdre knows about irony and she knows that he doesn't. It's not him but the dream itself that keeps cueing her. Had she glanced down and found strings attached to her limbs, she could not be more certain. She obeys the dream's desire for her to get up and go into the bathroom. For the first time in her life, she is truly sure of something. This is that when all things are possible, nothing at all matters.

---

Hours ago her mother checked and found her bed empty. She woke Deirdre's father and he called the police, though they could do nothing about a missing adult until the forty-eight-hour clock had ground down. It was nearly noon when Deirdre arrived home. The two of them were still in their bathrobes, frozen in waiting. Looking into their faces, she noticed for the first time that they had grown old. They had brought her into the world, had shared life with her, and she had always felt that she had nothing of consequence to share with them. Until that moment.

She had been sneaking out of the house for some time, prostituting herself in Harlem, where the customers and the vice squad were by necessity gentler than anywhere else in the city. The previous night, she told her parents, she had gotten very drunk and had fallen asleep in the room she rented in order to rent herself. Stylianos, though surely dead because, for ages, she felt him so, came to her in a dream. In death he had grown younger—as young as he was when they first met. His thin, taut arms and chest were slackened and his genitals shrunken, as though in embarrassment. After love, she washed away, with witch hazel, the feline mask he was hiding under. His face came clean except for one stubborn burn streak, which ran from his forehead to the bridge of his nose. The sight of his face roused her from the dream and she woke to find that her dream and the morning were one and the same. Stylianos's features raced through time to catch up to hers. Suddenly they were on parity: two thirty-seven-year-olds locked in a pietà embrace in a shallow bathtub.

His kiss had drugged her, she told her mother and father. There were stretches of the night she could not account for. At sunrise, she and Stylianos heard Death knocking feebly at the door and begging entrance in the voice of an old man. They lacked the strength to answer, shivering there together in the tub.

Her father asked if she had been robbed.

"No," she said, "I got paid."

She showed him the money.

---

Father Carney came to interview her. She was very forthcoming, and he asked, in the interests of tranquility, that she stop telling her story to the neighbors. Her father drove her to the Our Lady of Perpetual Mercy Home in Elmira. She was told that she had to be confined to the grounds and kept under constant surveillance in case a second miracle should happen to her. For fourteen years she told the head doctor and the patient sisters the same story over and over again. At the beginning of the fifteenth year, the funding cuts from the Archdiocese were so severe that they had no choice but to believe her.

When they told her that she was cured, she said, "Cured like a goddamn ham. You've given me so many drugs, I'll never spoil."

Prior to her release, her parents redeemed their life insurance policies and moved to Elmira to be near to her. They fashioned a room for her in their new house that was much like her lodgings at Our Lady. It had autumnal green wallpaper, a wooden crucifix mounted above the bed, and iron bars on the window. Her mother and father died within six months of each other. For years to follow, she would remark to herself that they would have lived longer if the three of them, alone together and individually there in that house, could have somehow found something to say to each other.

---

The birdbath water is leaden in her belly. She stalls on the back steps as the neighbor's porch light switches on, highlighting the ions of rain, silver against the darkness. She knows now that she must go into the house. She could stand naked in the rain all night and live to see the sun come up, but she would have to do it with her eyes closed. The silver rain reminds her of hope, and hope is an addiction she parted with long ago. In her hallway, there is a goalie's mask with black tiger stencilings running down the length of its face. She never fails to touch it as she goes by. She steps into the bathroom and shudders into her mother's robe. She stands there, waiting to see if she will have to vomit up the memory of Stylianos's skin. She looks deeply into the mirror; she grins at herself.

She says, "I hope he's this old and ugly when I meet him."

She raises her head and addresses the ceiling.

"I didn't mean You, Lord."

**The Pyramid**   Life changed everything but her name; matrimony, for her, was a matter of body and soul and it had nothing whatsoever to do with names. Her gypsy husband had shed his long ago—it was unspoken even by his brother and cousin—but he relished the sound of hers. He would have her recite it endlessly and he would ask to hear the stories of the templates, the ancestors and the adoptive saints, and knowing what he knew, he could no more ask her to add his name to hers than he could bid her to alter a prayer. In truth neither she nor her husband ever prayed; when they felt the need for reverence, one or the other of them would speak her name.

Her name was Altagracia Fatima Libanesa Maria Irenes de Concepcion Esmerelda Bonifacio Faustina Santostefano de

Girona Zangrillo y Dileones. Her life long, it assured her that there was a validity to her existence, real and true antecedents to her identity, long preceding her birth and christening. There were, for instance, her Catalan mercenary forebears, luckless in the end despite the poetry of their own names, the intercessions of their saints, and the loyalty of their wives. Men so celebrated for their bravery in distant conflicts that could not have concerned them nor their families in the least that, before the war blew it to ruins, Altagracia was able to read about them in the Municipal Library. Men, this the history books failed to mention, whose Catholicism failed to allow for the balm of irony, so they wept while their wives gave thanks when their sons ran off to avoid conscription. And these men were only reputed to her, though they were no less vivid for having been glimpsed only in tintypes. In her own memory there was a skeletal, gray-bearded great-grandfather physician with a fondness for something in his medical bag that made his eyes shine like those of the glasswork saints in the cathedral loft—she knew for a fact that, oftentimes, desperate mothers would plead with him through clenched teeth to turn his waxen face to the wall, and that his medical practice thrived owing to the rumor that death, if not exactly afraid of him, was at least leery of looking him in the eye.

Whereas they would have whispered such a thing when he was seventy, frail, and hard of hearing, though fit enough to subsidize them all, they said it out loud and in his presence when he was over eighty and presumed to be stone-deaf. He had outlived his health, his addiction, his fortune, and those of his children who had loved him. Altagracia's own mother and father were found yards apart on the seashore at the dawn of a day that would be blackened from a lineage of calendars that hung in the family parlor. On that day, they would dress Altagracia in black and she, not knowing half of the true story, would watch the sky for some omen of inclusive finality—rainfall, on that day, would exhilarate her.

On his deathbed, her great-grandfather told the family that he did not wish to die without having seen Barcelona, forgetting that he had trained there as a young man and had attended numerous medical forums and libidinal conventions in the city over the years. His youngest daughter—Altagracia's grandmother—humored him by packing a haversack and leaving it where he could easily see it. At the moment of his death, she picked up the bag and told Altagracia to follow her. Realizing that her grandmother was serious, she asked the old woman if she didn't, at least, want to stay for the funeral.

Alluding to his legend, her grandmother said, "Papa has enough dirt on him already."

---

The two of them arrived in Barcelona during the Holy Week, and in their own very dignified way they invited charity by sitting upon the bone-white steps of the seminary building along Las Ramblas, doing and saying little for the whole of Good Friday, Holy Saturday, and the better part of Easter Sunday. They watched the plaster icons parade by; one rhinestone-eyed Madonna Blanca caused the old woman to cross herself several times over, far more in fear than in deference, and both of them decided that the Easter costumes and reverential stage properties of Barcelona were fit for the Fool's Day procession of their native village. The meals kept coming, some of them on platters draped with fine lace, just as they would be, in those days, for the visiting prelates and their entourages. These meals were lavish to the point of comedy and seldom had Altagracia eaten paella that did not bespeak the age of the sea and never had she a full bota of wine to share with only her grandmother, who turned to the proffered cinnamon tea when her head began to hum. There were, in addition, ample pillows to smooth the stone steps and quilted blankets to warm their sleep. In Altagracia's memory, the charitable, however, would remain as faceless as dream ghouls, perhaps because no one among them thought to offer shelter— not on the day of Christ's dying, not on the daylong interval of His absence, and not at the hour of His rebirth.

Her grandmother did not rise from the pillows, not even to urinate. Altagracia's own trips to the "water closet" became more frequent and lengthy and they drew severe scolding from the old woman, who was complaining of stomach cramps and wanted her company. Though she loved her grandmother, by Sunday every single soul was either in church or home with their shutters tight, biding happily in their own quiet acts of heresy, and the Plaza de Cataluna, with its six- and seven-foot chess piece statuary and its grillwork-trimmed tributary side streets, seemed to belong to her and her alone. It was sundown when she returned to the steps and found her grandmother lying back with a blanket bundled over her face. She looked at the sky and saw that there was almost a half-hour of fragile light left to the day. This was not to be wasted. She was turning to leave when she noticed her grandmother's hands, clear of either side of the blanket, and crabbed into fists, the knuckles without blood, showing bone. Certainly it was an indelicacy to allow one's grandmother to lie like that in public. The old woman was a dead sleeper; more than once, in their common bed back home, Altagracia had changed the disgraced sheets without waking her. She did not hesitate to unfurl those hands and, prying at the right one, she pricked her finger on one of the unkept nails—in reflex, she brought her hand to her mouth and she tasted blood. She knew then and it would not have been necessary for her to turn and see the mounted guardia, who had originally covered the body, return, nor for her to make out the white-gowned medical crew on the horizon; she knew that her grandmother had taken the only shelter offered, the only one available. The officer of the guard directed her to come down the steps. When she reached him he was looking into the dying sun, undoubtedly damning his honor and duty to the blackest hell for the words he found himself speaking in encounters such as this one. However, to her, it appeared as though he was every bit as inattentive as the horse beneath him—both of them were looking in the opposite direction and chewing air.

"Who is that?" the guardia asked.

"My grandmother," she said.

"Do you know that she is dead?"

Everyone in her family who had mattered to her was now also dead and he had said it in a strident tone, as though dead relations were somehow uncommon and worthy of his particular scorn.

"She has every right to be dead," she said.

---

Before leaving the village her grandmother had the presence of mind to pack Altagracia's baptismal certificate in that haversack lately present at two fatalities, and the date printed on the document made her eligible for the Our Lady of the Interventions Orphanage, though only for the three months it was going to take for her to reach the age of sixteen. In former times, a maid among the constabulary told her, the cut-off age extended to eighteen and the institution found itself rabid with the curse of fully matured hormones. The church had no remedy for this, save exorcisms and ice baths. She was brought before the orphanage's Abbess by a delegation from the guard, ten of them crowding into the sandalwood-spiced office and, cowed by the sorrowful tapestries on the walls, they explained the girl's pitiable circumstances in the same hushed tones they would have used in the confessional. The entire time that they were speaking to her, the Abbess toyed with a strip of linen, binding it and unbinding it in either palm. The girl guessed this to be a self-ordained penance, since she was certain that the blood of Christ (what else would the Mother Superior be wiping away?) was the color of air—she'd seen it penetrate sacred wine without darkening the hue.

Altagracia, at fifteen years and nine months, stood a full six feet and wore burnished blonde tresses, grazing the root of her spine—she was so lovely in a willowy, supine manner that she made the Abbess feel like an orphan; the Abbess knew well that if she had the girl's beauty she would have little need for God's affection and favor, and so she thanked the guardia and remanded Altagracia to her underlings. She then sat back and did absolutely nothing while great vistas of spite opened up all around her. The girl was given a few rudimentary Bible lessons and then asked to identify such dramatis personae as Zerubbabel, Johanan, and Shechaniah. She could not recall any of these people, but in her private mind she obsessed over the injunction in Leviticus that forbade her to look upon the nakedness of her father. She wished with all of her heart that he were alive so that she could know what all the fuss was about and she wondered if fatherhood physically disfigured a man—if stretch marks could be common to both sexes. When she stood mute to repeated questioning by the nuns, she was accused of blaspheming in her heart and duly paddled in front of the class. Later, at lunch, she was afraid to leave a glass of obviously tainted milk undrunk, and that evening she cowered in terror at having vomited up the Eucharist following mass.

She was kept waiting until near to midnight in a windowless cellar. The door unbolted and a sputtering goose oil lamp revealed the Mother Superior and her aide Sister Martellato, who was allowed to go about in trousers. The flicker of their forms in the inconstant light had Altagracia halfway convinced that the pair of them had died that day and that their ghosts had decided to continue antagonizing her. They told her that they had come to look for telltale signs of her bondage to the devil and demanded that she take off her clothes. All her life she had heard of her debt to the dead and now she found that she could refuse them nothing, not even an indecency. The sight of Altagracia's blistered bottom startled the Abbess. Sister Martellato scurried up the stairs and soon came back with reassurances that the girl had, indeed, been spanked and that her rear end was not actually festering with some dark stigmata, as the Abbess had been quick to assume. They went on to find three tiny moles that formed a triangular pattern in her armpit, but neither of them could recall a corresponding link in Revelations. The Abbess didn't know what to think and she let the matter ride upon the opinion of her aide.

Sister Martellato said, "Let's cut her hair, trim her nails, and move her bowels."

The Abbess cracked the door a precious few inches in order to holler up for a pair of greenhouse sheers, a patch of sandpaper, and jar of preserved prune jam. In legend, which was entirely of Altagracia's own making, and which remained irrefutable in the vulture coop that the war would later make of that orphanage, Altagracia sprinted naked through the cleft in the door and she was unmolested in her run to freedom because the other sisters thought, as had the Mother Superior, that her delicate posterior was marked with the demonic equivalent of the tail of a comet.

---

In Barcelona in those days, there were several artists' quarters, each of them equally fruitful and desperate; the largest lay in the southeastern corner of the city and it was known as "Africa." The residents there were not predominantly dark-skinned, as one might expect; it was called Africa, rather, because it was thought to be barbarous and unknowable. The provincial landlords of the neighborhood had bought their properties through mountebank agents at state auctions and they were wary of venturing into the district, even in pursuit of their rental fees. They feared not so much being set upon and robbed, for incidence of this was almost unheard of; it was the threat of the evil eye or some other rumored and shadowy viral contaminant that set them on edge. This gave rise to a phenomenon known as "spring cleaning"; each April, bands of country youths in the employ of the landlords would arrive in Africa armed with broken-off stanchions and up-to-date account ledgers.

Altagracia could not have known any of this. She was simply given a half-loaf of blue-speckled bread wrapped in newsprint and, eating what she could of the bread, she saw an advertisement seeking "Ladies of breeding and character who must have good posture and will work for room and board." She showed the newspaper to several people on the street and they either frosted and went away or warned her not to go near the printed address. A sympathetic liveryman, who thought that he was reuniting her with loved ones, finally agreed to take her there in his mule cart and he was happy to accept her smile as payment. Entering the building she was frightened. The liveryman told her of anarchists who had leveled entire city blocks in order that they be given leave not to bathe and to fornicate during church services. She climbed to the limbo between the sixth and seventh floors; she stopped, feeling a moss beginning to grow in the seams of her toes, exposed as they were in her frayed sandals. The dust upon each of the steps had a quality of tamped fur to it; it was only the multiple footprints that convinced her that she was not treading upon a decomposing carpet. Her second guess was explosive powder—she had never seen such a substance, but in view of what the liveryman had said, she did not know what else the lush, gray residue on the steps could be; it could very well be leaking through the air from the enclosed and numbered cells all around her. The silence in the hall had an air of combustibility to it, as though the mere breath of a stranger would be enough to ignite the charge. She sealed her lungs and backtracked upon the balls of her feet, and then, unaccountably, the sun knifed through the window on the landing and the air about her ankles was afire with crystal flecks and crushed diamonds. Her heart was in her mouth and she rocketed ahead of the swooshing fireball that licked at her heels and painted a chilly streak along her spine.

The two brothers and the one cousin who shared the rooms opposite the stairwell on the seventh floor were Romany folk from Cadiz. Their borrowed name was de Santangel and they kept the hour of siesta as religiously as the Sabbath. They had spent their childhoods in the open air and they were not as yet sold on the idea that unstirred air was not always malarial. The door and the windows remained wide open. To guard them in their sleep, they relied upon the fabulists, who spread stories of vengeful gypsy ghosts and their clandestine taste for the blood of Christian children. Resurreccion (their given names were also on loan) was the youngest and he slept at the right corner of the bed. He was dreaming that he was in a country where it was customary for both the male and female to don matching guillotinesman burnooses during the sexual act and he found this much to his liking, thinking it the logical extension of the masked ball. The problem was that his dream partner's kneecaps were deep in the twin plates of his breast and he felt his lungs flattened like two shrinking inner tubes. Speechless and breathless, he pushed himself upward and parted the liquid curtain of the dream, just as Altagracia galloped up to the backboard of the bed with the cry of fire cocked on her tongue. She took a single look at his red-rimmed eyes and at the crimson shadow that flowed from his torso to his cheeks.

She said, "Fire?"

Still half in the dream he thought that she was offering to light his postcoital cigarette—he abstained from smoking after sex because Romany men of the era still prevailed upon God with burnt offerings; he was afraid that the Almighty might misread the vaporous signal and look down upon his nakedness, expecting to see a roasting lamb.

"No, thank you," he said.

She did not hear him because she was focusing on the dangling unicycle, which swayed above the bed in perfect sync with the groggy arc his shoulders were making. She had seen unicycles, of course, but in her mind they were not such things as to hang over the bed. The space above sleep, in her grandfather's house, was reserved for the crucifix alone. She was still certain that she was among anarchists and, without articulating it even in thought, she suspected that the unicycle might be some sort of tantric eye, its cylindrical spokes storing the radium of the moon. Not wanting to be in the room with it, him, or them, and still not courageous enough to brave those steps, she began to dance in place while he rose from the bed and made a vain attempt to cup his genitals—she made an equally vain attempt not to look.

"Have a cup of tea, won't you?" he said, not yet realizing that she wasn't the hooded paramour of his recent dream.

Bautismo sat up in the center of the bed before she could reply. He was cousin to the two brothers and, from earliest childhood, a valued hedge against fratricide. He asked what time it was and Resurreccion said, "Never mind," without looking at him or at the clock. Bautismo fell back to sleep. He tried gallantly to make conversation, all the while getting neither yea nor nay from the transfixed girl. He asked her to excuse his two bowed legs and he catalogued their breakage since the accursed day long ago when he had taken his older brother Crucifixion's dare and walked the length of their encampment's clothesline. He held out his arms before her; the left was the longer and the straighter of the two. He had her tap at the crook between the forearm and biceps of his right arm. She jerked her hand back, having knocked wood, and he laughed and said, "Come in." She found herself laughing despite her fear. He asked, quite formally, for permission to put his pants on. She told him, by all mean, yes, and he was satisfied that she wasn't even silently unsatisfied. His honor intact, he dressed to the whistling of the teapot. He told her of "The Pyramid," the final act in the theater of the wire that he and his brother and cousin performed each evening in the Plaza de Cataluna. Shorter and stouter than either of the others, Crucifixion would roll to the center of the suspended steel cord atop his unicycle. Then Bautismo and Resurreccion would approach from either side and, in tandem, they would mount the twin ledges of Crucifixion's shoulders while the unicycle's rotund wheel treaded all but naked air—grown men in the crowd, Resurreccion insisted, would look their mortality in the eye for the first time and it was they, he said, none but the brave, who would swoon.

She asked if he was afraid of death. He raised his hands to gesture and she was sure that he was going to cross himself, as her grandmother would have done, but instead he drew a straight and even line in the air. He told her that none of them had fallen in three years and that the day that they had ceased to cover the floor of the Plaza with bedding was the day that the de Santangels had finally taken off their diapers. Furthermore, he and his brother Crucifixion had now made their peace with the counsel of their cousin Bautismo and this though they had fought even previous to infancy. Why, Crucifixion, a year-and-a-half his brother's senior, anticipated the rivalry by scrawling a curse upon the wall of their mother's womb and signed not his name but the order of his birth to it; it was only in the covenant of the wire that they learned to trust and respect each other.

Crucifixion woke to the bird song of the teapot. He sat up in bed with his eyes cooking in their sockets, and Altagracia felt like ducking her head because those eyes were so closely set, dark, and deep that just looking at him was like hurdling down a narrow and endless underpass. He spoke to his younger brother with a strained patience, thanking Resurreccion for the compliment, but, all the same, his shoulders and arms were not fashioned from granite—if he thought that he could sustain the combined weights of Resurreccion, Bautismo, and this whooping crane that he had allowed into their flat, then his intelligence level called into question the very virtue of their common mother. Addressing Altagracia directly, he suggested that she might find more suitable employment in the countryside where the toilers of the earth had need for her type in order to keep the crows from their corn, and although he didn't wish to seem rude, when her cup of tea was finished, her welcome was likewise over and done.

It was only then that Resurreccion remembered the advertisement and their agreed upon need to crown The Pyramid with a female assistant. He, likewise, had little desire to support the weight of such a beanstalk while ten feet above the Plaza (that was their ceiling then), but his sense of valor provoked him into speaking out for her.

"Crucifixion," he said, "since you make so much of her height, be so good as to come out of the bed and show your own shortcoming."

Luckily, Crucifixion's trembling roused Bautismo and he sensed the familiar odor of bated blood in the air. He directed Resurreccion to take the girl for a walk while he pacified the elder brother. Resurreccion readily agreed, telling Altagracia to bring her teacup, they were not going far, but instead of making for the door he climbed out of the window, his teacup balanced on top of his head. She had no choice but to follow, since the black beam from the eyes of the elder brother was soiling her dress. The ledge circumvented the entire building and he insisted on giving her the full spherical tour. The tea was spiced with herbs she could not identify, but she thought that it tasted a bit like tree bark. She clung to the memory of playing in the trees as a child and this helped her keep her distance from fear— this along with his voice, which served as an aural harness, wrapping her around with vines of outrageous lies, telling of feats of brothel prowess in his tender, subteen years, of the illegitimates he had sired to slumming duchesses, and of how the dark-skinned Virgin of Monserrat had taken his original innocence in a vision without so much as mussing her umber halo in the act. Resurreccion now knew that his siesta's dream had indeed been only a phantom of sleep, but he was beginning to feel sleepy once more. He reclined on the building's shelf and he told her that she was beautiful. He said that there could be no shame between the two of them, not here in the great blue bed of God.

With a stone in her heart, she positioned her feet so that she could kick him if he moved one bare inch toward her. The sky darkened and the sun, which had been nettling the back of her neck for the longest while, cooled instantly. She looked up and the south wind parted her hair, lifting either end of the mane like two silken wings. He was looking, so she tried to smooth her hair; her palm came away burning. She looked to the sky and she saw the color of flight: a vivid breathless blue—she had seen this color before in robin's eggs and in flower beds, and once in the vulva of a seashell, but she had never before noticed it above her head. She glanced and saw her shadow fading to vapor upon the stone of the building's façade as the sky altered its complexion. The hairs on the back of her neck tingled as though in a rain of astringent and she felt a lightness she had never known previously while awake.

She was afraid until that moment. She thought them fallen angels, retaining only their powers of levitation and the abiding wickedness that had obviously cost them paradise, but in this lightness there was a falling away, a buoyancy, a suspension of judgment, and even a suspension of the logic of gravity. As the rain came down, it was easy for her to imagine walking the air to be like dreaming while awake, like dying while alive; she rose to her tiptoes and in a flash she knew what it felt like to have one foot in this world and the other in the world beyond. She turned to tell Resurreccion, but he was crouching on his heels at the blade of the ledge. He had his hands held out to the sky.

---

They did not invite her to stay nor to leave, and after years of living with them, she decided that they did not realize they had the authority to get rid of her, just as they could not have conceived of expelling the hardships of winter, memory, or kinship—they were all three eligible young men, yet they seemed never to think of marriage since life, for them, was something of a betrothal with all things, for better, for worse. She became part of their random plan; she chased the mildew from the corners of their floors, she scoured the carbon from the bottoms of their cooking vessels; she would watch, each nightfall, as they struggled into their pastel harlequin skins, Resurreccion looping the coil of mountaineer's wire, like an armored collar, around his neck, and each of them toting fifty-pound balancing beams. They would march out the door single file beneath a length of tarp they had cut from the blanket of a ship in the harbor to serve as their protective net. She would look through the window and see the amputated tail of a dragon tottering down the street, watching for rain, and imagining the slickness of the wire and the peril of the wind. At times like these, she would know beyond doubt that they were out of their minds and that this was the reason they were capable of getting out of their bodies and walking through the air in their incarnate souls.

She got rid of the few applicants to the newspaper ad by simply telling them what they were wanted for. For a short while, the boys employed a drunken, cross-eyed sailor's wife whose husband shunned life in the same hemisphere as her. For the promise of a bota, she would scramble across the wire in the clownishly wide flypaper shoes that they had bought from a retiring chimney cleaner. They thought her uproarious for all of a moment and then they began to grumble, each in confidence to Altagracia, that she was undermining the dignity of their act. The prospect of an entire vineyard could not induce her to mount the summit of The Pyramid, and her association with them came to an abrupt end one afternoon while Bautismo was teaching her to turn an arabesque. She fell, breaking both her arms and uncrossing her eyes.

Bautismo told Altagracia that he could forgive the woman's drunkenness; what he could not forgive and what was tantamount to suicide, not to mention homicide, was the fact that she had looked into his eyes during the lesson. Equilibrium upon the wire lay not in the balancing rod, nor in the positioning of the feet, nor even in the mindset of the walker; it was in the eyes—they must be locked like a dead man's, straight ahead and focused on nothing. Eye contact, Bautismo told her, invited the misfortune of gravity.

She took this to heart as she practiced each evening, in secret, upon a two-by-four-inch plank of wood. With her eyes open and unseeing, she learned the lay of the narrow board as thoroughly as the ear acquires a repeated song. Simple striding came easily, but the glissades and entrechats she had set her heart upon tried her patience to no end. She often had to ignore the boys when they would come home from the Plaza and ask her why she was limping. When she'd mastered the practice plank, she moved on to the flagpole at the north end of their building. The iron staff sported an all-weather wardrobe—one week loyal to the exiled monarchy and the next heralding the rebel army. One particular fortnight, the pole wore a skirt of bleached lunar rubrics against a cavernous black background, and Altagracia liked this outfit best; the possession of the governmental apparatus seemed as earthly perilous and cosmically peripheral as that flag seemed to presume. Standing on the pole, she would tune her breathing to the rhythmic drifting of the clouds and she would experience an ethereality few individuals know following their births. Without effort she rerouted her fear to the above rather than the below—her terror was of falling upward and entering the same sodden whirlpool that the night's constellations were eternally damned to.

---

It was evening in the Plaza and they had strung their wire, as always, between the two imported poplars, which had been naked and lifeless for generations. Resurreccion was upright on the wire, his hair matted and a shade darker than she knew it rightfully to be; his face was shining. To his right, Crucifixion signaled from his unicycle and Resurreccion released his balancing pole. He stepped from the wire. The crowd crushed closer and stole the air from her lungs. She saw his hand flash in the air an instant before he caught the iron cord and swung upward, in an arc, as though he would dip his feet into the clouds. The crowd loosened, she breathed once more; he stood on the wire and kissed his fingers. Bautismo, likewise, dropped his balancing pole while Crucifixion kept hold of his. The three of them met at the center of the wire and Crucifixion straddled the unicycle, as still as a pillar, the cord beneath them hammocking in the wind. Bautismo stepped onto his shoulder and the two bodies bobbed like some allegoric fable set adrift. When the wire was calm once more, Resurreccion started to mount his cousin's other shoulder and Altagracia turned her eyes away and pleaded and thrashed until the diffident crowd cut a path for her. Her hands and her feet were slippery; her fingernails could not penetrate the crust of the poplar tree—it was her taut thighs that did most of the climbing. She could not have fathomed the electric chill of the wire, nor the booming silence, which was not silence at all, but the condition of being scrutinized by a hundred uncomprehending strangers, their absorption dispersing the street sounds. She wanted to call out to the de Santangels and tell them not to move, as though they would have, and not to look, as though they were not already seeing her, although each of them kept his eyes averted.

The gravest lesson was the umbilical nature of the wire—it startled her to think that the threat of mortality had rounded the four of them into one body, even though this was what she wanted—this was the fullness of intimacy she had long craved with Resurreccion, to share even his blood ties and his unblinking and blind view of death. She tried not to look at them but she could not help it. In the tightness of their mouths, she saw that they too were afraid and she felt a thermal flowering, a rush of certitude that was to save all of their lives that evening. She moved forward and stepped onto Crucifixion's shoulder. Resurreccion's feet, her stepping-stones, were cold, as she expected, the rag around his hand turning crimson, the wire having cut through the cloth. Consoling words formed in her mind, but she knew that if she spoke them, the wind alone would hear her. She kept climbing and the wire molded into a perfect v-shape. She was in too great a hurry to wait for it to right itself. Resurreccion seemed to be compressing, his damp thigh and knotted shoulder bowing to her like a fanciful staircase in a dream. She stood to her full height, straddling Resurreccion on the right and Bautismo on the left. The wind blew through her legs; she shivered on the inside, and two parallel columns of sweat burst from her hairline—she feared that they would salt her eyes. She raised her hand to her forehead and heard a murmur spreading below; the crowd thought she was saluting them and they considered this a sacrilege. Just moments before, they had knelt as one in prayer.

There were revelers outside their apartment's window through the evening. She kept her distance from Crucifixion, but having been given no say in what had taken place, he now found nothing to say to anyone. Resurreccion had little to say as well, but when his brother and cousin had apparently gone to sleep and the celebrants had finally stumbled home to their hangovers, he entered the alcove where she'd lain alone since that first night and for the second time that evening they trembled together in what was initially fear, then elation.

The Colonel's name was Zobel; his headquarters were within the requisitioned Hotel Mariposa and he held Crucifixion captive in what were once the concierge's private rooms. Crucifixion was ill-advisedly drinking with some Nationalist soldiers and he told them the story of how, two years previous and shortly after the wedding of his brother Resurreccion to a headstrong waif named Altagracia, he suffered a fall during a performance and broke his arm. A magistrate and his staff of clerks rushed to the infirmary with the ears and tail of a defeated bull, slain only blocks away and moments apart from Crucifixion's mishap. He wept in his infirmary bed and insisted that the remnants of the beast be burnt; he considered the gesture such an act of evil charity that he feared his luck to be forever contaminated, and he swore never to perform again.

The soldiers needed bodies for the morning terror—they were by then too drunk and complacent to beat down barricaded doors and rouse the sleeping. For months the men of the city woke to riotous church bells and were made to go out into the street to overturn the dead. On more than one occasion, brother had overturned brother, or father had drawn the duty of over-turning his son. As they stood crying over the corpses, a commander would order one of his men to shoot in order to affect a "family reunion." In light of what he had told them, Crucifixion was a natural candidate for the morning ritual; to the drunken soldiers, it was obvious that he was unemployed, effeminate in spirit despite his broad back and solid limbs, a coward, and also an unreconstructed gypsy. He was taken to a field on the outskirts of the city and made to stand with the others who had been unfortunate that night. At the command, he turned his back and walked away from the soldiers, two weeping men on either side of him, and listening for the crack of the rifles, he lost consciousness, and then heard the shots in a dream. He arrived back in the Plaza with a bloody scalp and a concussion; he stood up from the dead truck and approached Colonel Zobel and asked what had happened. It would not be apparent for several days that the bullet had also scattered his sanity.

Colonel Zobel had hung deserters younger than the least oldest of his own sons, but it seemed to him that he had done this in another war and perhaps in another lifetime. The city was sure to fall to the Leftists soon and he and his command would be retreating, to where he knew not. For him the war was ending and he was not so sure he couldn't say the same about his life—he resided in his thoughts and he watched his actions with the interests of an outsider; he longed to be entertained. The Colonel allowed Resurreccion and Bautismo to visit Crucifixion. The concierge's bedroom at the Mariposa was now a garden of candles since the chaplain of Zobel's company was not actually a religious man, despite being an ordained priest; he was instead a superstitious man, convinced that sacramental candles quarantined the demons of madness. He replaced the tallows every twelve hours, gibbering in Latin as he moved about the room. Crucifixion recognized his brother and his cousin. They told him what the Colonel had said: that the price of Crucifixion's freedom was a performance—in the Gothic quarter, along the disused bridge with the single pillared support in the center— the one the locals called La Cruz. He nodded as though he truly understood and he gave Resurreccion and Bautismo his blessing, his forefinger sketching an x in the air. He asked that they not séance him awake ever again since, in the land where he had gone to, fatigue was not cured by sleep and he was too weary to bear the weight of their sadness. He promised to dream of them often.

---

On the night of the performance, Altagracia stood on the bridge with her head upon Resurreccion's shoulder and she found herself staring at the wire that was strung between the riggings. The retreating sun colored both the wire and the latticing cables a shade of peach and gold, and the patterns of the webbed metal, added in vain to the decaying bridge centuries after it was built, were echoed in the cloud tissues in the sky. Death seemed as familiar and nonchalant as a blank mirror. Within seconds, she came to her senses, momentarily alarmed at the burning in her stomach and the crush of her husband's hand over her mouth. A lieutenant came forward to ask what she had been laughing at. She said, "Nothing."

There was no unicycle to be found. Crucifixion, operating perhaps on memory and perhaps on instinct, walked to the center of the wire and squatted like a man who would defecate in the road. He offered the two other men his shoulders to climb on. Altagracia, standing at the edge of the wire, feeling the vibrations of the weight of Bautismo and Resurreccion settling upon Crucifixion, hearing the applause of the officers and remarking to herself that it sounded like small-arms fire, took a single step toward them. Her husband turned his head, but did not look into her eyes; he shook his head no. Crucifixion shifted his weight from the right foot to the left, and she felt the wire buckle and rode it out with one of her slippers in the air, the heft of her balancing pole tipping her body off-balance like an oar caught in a current. She let the heavy baton go, hoping that it would kill one of the officers below.

For the remainder of her life, she would have slept much better if there had been a flash of eye contact, an instant of goodbye, between her and Resurreccion, but just as there was no guardrail, no banister on that bridge, there was nothing in the moment for her to hold onto—there was not even the lodestone of blame to assign. Feeling another current through the wire, she looked just in time to see Resurreccion and Bautismo fall from Crucifixion's shoulders. Crucifixion turned to her, so careless in his footing now that she had to spread her arms to steady herself. Death seemed a foregone conclusion, so she broke the sole commandment of her craft; she looked into his eyes. She saw heat—the very same glassy bonfire that burnt in her great-grandfather's eyes in life and in death, and she was so frightened that she wanted to live.

Twenty years later, she returned to Barcelona, having published a best-selling book about her life during the war, although she was never able to read it—it was ghostwritten in French and she never bothered with the language, except to learn the hours of the day, the days of the week, the weeks of the month, and the months of the year. She once purchased a television set in hopes of expanding her vocabulary, but within a week she got rid of it, deciding that if she really wanted to eavesdrop on the private lives of gray-toned phantoms, then memory was the better medium. In Barcelona, no one spoke of the war, but for the occasional toast to the Generalissimo's victory and his continued good health. Otherwise people were quick to change the subject when she mentioned those times. She asked Fortunata, her travel guide who was barely born when Altagracia left the country, to take her to the old Knights of Santiago Graveyard. She learned long ago that it was here that the rebels had buried Resurreccion and Bautismo to the accompaniment of artillery. Fortunata secured a car and an escort of two surly adolescents in Italian suits. They were given permission to remain in the burial grounds for half an hour.

Entering the graveyard, she saw a great brass wheel with spokes of silver-colored wire, elevated high above the stones and the terra-cotta saints. She found herself trembling, but Fortunata only smiled and the youths looked away.

"We tell the tourists that they were gypsy test pilots," Fortunata said. "Martyred angels."

Altagracia sat down on the grass and closed her eyes, and when she opened them, one of the youths was standing over her, tapping at his watch face. She went and stood under the brass wheel and looked at the ground at her feet. She saw that there were three burial mounds. Printed upon a panel of varnished wood were the names of all three de Santangels and according to the panel they had all died on the same day. She asked if the soldiers had shot Crucifixion. Through the years, she had not heard a word from or about him, and in her memoir her ghostwriter allowed him the dignity of walking away along the bridge in the opposite direction, as Altagracia did. Fortunata said, yes, of course, Crucifixion was scratched on the skull by the eye of a bullet; he passed out, woke to rain of soil upon his shirtfront, and stood and asked the gravedigger to drive him home.

Altagracia said, "And after that?"

"He was mad. They had to put him in jail."

"But how did he die?"

"He fell," Fortunata whispered, as though the obvious had suddenly become suspect.

"No," Altagracia said, "he climbed down. I saw him. He was alive."

Fortunata took her arm and began to lead her back to the car. "Señora," she said, "you are the one who lived."

The next day Fortunata took her to the biblioteca and they located a newspaper account on microfiche with a photo of the three bodies under a common blanket and another of Altagracia in her harlequin suit with a military colonel's jacket around her shoulders—her younger image looked into the camera in disbelief and it startled her to realize that this was the present look she must have been wearing on her face. She did not read the news article, or the captions beneath the photographs. She asked her guide to make arrangements for her return to Paris as soon as possible.

Someone else in her pension was also departing, or perhaps they had just arrived; there was a celebration in the next room with festive music from a phonograph—music with a rhythmic cadence to it, unidentifiable despite its familiarity, keeping her awake, stoking her curiosity, and trying her patience. Then the party ended so abruptly that the silence made her feel abandoned; she'd long past given up on the idea of sleep. She switched on the bedside radio and through the static she heard a voice call her name. She turned off the radio and listened, but there was nothing. Again, she turned on the radio and the voice called her. The voice was Bautismo's and he said that he would tell her a story to make her sleep. There was a princess who became a widow. The emptiness at the end of her life caused her to seek out an enchantress. After drinking from a gurgling rain barrel, she set about living her life over, this time in reverse. She saved her royal husband from his death, thus dooming him to an inverted birth and an eternal limbo of preexistence, which, said Bautismo, is a prince's lot in any case, and she grew younger, more beautiful, and graciously left her prince when the demands of his puberty proved too much for her. She married into a family of acrobats. When she took off her crown and her jewels, she found that she could walk the air just as they did. She and her new family traveled above the clouds and had adventures with highlanders who had biblical names and plumes of feathers sprouting from their spines. In the highlands, air-walking was thought to be nothing special, so the princess and her new husband resolved to learn to fly.

She was thirsty and she asked Bautismo's voice for a cup of water. From the shadows, Crucifixion brought the cup to her. She looked at it in what light she could find; the surface was not bubbling; it tasted like water. She asked Crucifixion if he had truly fallen from the wire that day. He told her to go look through the window. She asked him what she would see, but he would say nothing more.

Trying to stay ahead of the dream, she said, "Is it a wheel? Will I see a wheel?"

He pointed to the window.

There was no moon—the window's glass framed a sky the color of dread, blue-black with multiple swirls of gray-colored furor like an emotional x-ray. Then the sun rose so abruptly that it was as though a higher being had stepped into the sleeping room of the world and had carelessly switched on the light. Through the glass, she felt heat on her face. There were footsteps behind her. She said her husband's name and she turned around.

"How long have we been dead?" she asked him.

Resurreccion said, "Since before we were born."

**Slight Return**   The town knew how to throw a hotel, the posh ones downtown with the chalky white walls. Passing through with his circus, he would lie in bed and melt the top coats, reap the graffiti in the acrylic subsoil, repatriate the gold and ash throw rugs with the pop art racing stripes to the ocean floor, and watch the morning claim its fortune in the crystalline swan ash-trays—the suites so bright, sleek, and fragile, like the city. He left that last one, The Templar, when the driver, a peewee, came in and told him that it was time. He thought there was something off about the little man's uniform. It was a filling-station blue with a girl or a pimp's name—Chevron, was it?—stitched across the breast. All the chauffeurs in Europe wore morning coats; they called you "maestro."

"Too pussy for a tattoo?" Jimi asked.

The driver answered without parting his lips, a scratchy tape-reel voice, the purring of plastic wheels underneath. "Thank you, no. I hate cats."

He followed the driver out past the pool where women with rashes and multiple buttocks lay on foam carpets or in wicker recliners. "Morning," he called and his voice echoed around the courtyard, misquoted even here, even now. "Morphine, morphine, morphine," his voice said. He thought that they were going to take the Rolls Corniche, foam-white with the fountain's likeness, but no, it was the city bus with the stained-glass windows of vaporous blue and the patchwork-tiled floor, palled by the hue of the windows, spidered over by eternity, one rolling dead room.

"I don't have a guitar," he said as the driver folded the door after him.

That voice again and with a quarter-inch cleft in the mouth this time, his teeth like saw bits. "I don't have a road map."

"What's that supposed to—"

"We'll wing," the driver said and notched down his high chair. He laid his jackboot into the throttle. Jimi found himself hang gliding, giggling in the iron vestibule.

---

The town threw a mean freeway as well. This is what he remembered best, loved the most about Los Angeles—this broad, aimless broom stroke across the entire canvas of the city—a no-place running everywhere, a vascular channel colored the absolute shade of entropy (a saturated, spectral yellow), and not the least of its delights was its tonality, its fuzzbox clarion providing the perfect medium for thought. Although it had changed a great deal since last he'd been in town, which was—well, when? It was hard to say since he'd died twenty-one days ago and that was in London, definitely London; the consequence of an imbalance of quinalbarbitone, brallobarbitone, cannabis, cognac, and amphetamines. In the loopy hindsight of death, it seemed to Jimi that he'd allowed a cabal of zodiacal augurers into his bloodstream and died of an overdose of conjecture. He died on the road, albeit in an ambulance on a short tour to the Saint Mary Abbots Hospital in Kensington, and with the same plugged-in sensation that he was feeling now aboard the bus, the rolling wheels running a current up his spine. The ambulance attendant whispered, "Can I make you more comfortable?" directly into his ear, and though he felt like a live wire he lacked the oxygen—even with the plastic mask on—to answer or to swim to the threshold of sleep. The ambulance man's breath running up the viaduct, extinguishing the very last candle.

The strangest thing was that he was not so sure about an afterlife; it was so hard to think without a heartbeat. He was an electric blues deity, but death, as near as he could tell, was airy chamber music, lacking a rhythm section. Initially, it tickled the hell out of him to find himself conscious (he would have to call it that, lacking a keener translation) without vital signs. He even managed to pry loose a smile for Monika in the hospital cubicle and she stopped weeping for a second and snarled, "You bloody faker," at his corpse. He was certain that the trip would be linearly backward with each sour note soothed, each goodbye alleviated by hello. It was going to be a long lurch back to the womb with a headful of happy memories of the future. But then he dosed in London and woke in L.A., having missed his own funeral, although California wasn't first on the itinerary because he hadn't been on the West Coast since the summertime—where were Berlin, Stockholm, Honolulu, and New York? Was death a dream? Was life?

In however many months it had been, L.A.'d put TV on the expressway. There was a kid's show on—a variant of hide-and-seek with footage of blonde children wrestling with sheepdogs, toddling through elephant grass, some of them backlit by flaming birthday tablets while their shadows mimed on the wall. Apparently, these children were hiding in the streets and if you spotted them you were to phone the station or chant a telepathic spell given in shorthand, something like "W-w-w-dot-org-los-child." The iridescent sunset threw the screen's reflection onto the road and the children ran gleefully beneath the traffic. Jimi was in the back, lounging on one of the handicapped islands.

"How'd you get started bus driving?" he said, his voice reverberating up the aisle.

"I needed a night job."

"You're moonlighting? What's your regular gig?"

The driver considered it. "Chambermaid," he answered.

"Chamber—?"

"Waa' up?" a voice asked and Jimi looked to the opposite island. He saw a Geechee or a dark Okefenokee Swamp Indian maid wearing string braids and a wizard's scarves and satins. She held an enamel bowl with a pink hybrid rose floating in water that was as dense as developing fluid. Jimi looked for smoke or glitter dust in the air. His Cherokee grandmother, at eighty-odd, lit up her Kents off of the kitchen stove and slept away the afternoons on a blanket out by the tomato patch. She taught him a few words in the Mandarin of the Tribal Nations. On concert tours he'd startled the Native Mafiosi who would come backstage to claim kin—thickset, putty-nosed, momentarily speechless guys with names like Johnny Crow Dog or Jimmy Crack Corn.

"Tasata weya," Jimi said.

Her brow nettled prettily, the braids swaying, voiceless chimes.

"You'll pardon me, I only know a few words in Negro."

"That's all right, it's an attitude, not a language. You sew those dreads yourself?"

She served him a sharp look, her eyes feline both in their quickness and in their shade of almond. "My name is Lady Creti," she said. "Lady Donata Creti. I'm Bolognese and my family suffers from Neapolitan blood. Perhaps you'd like to refresh yourself?"

She handed him the rose bowl. There were tiny liquid beads pulsing deep in the twills of the flower. Jimi saw a blushing girl about to glow tears.

"How did you get here?"

"Old age, folly, by design, if you like."

"No, I meant—"

"I'd finished a fresco, an allegory of the Graces in the Cardinal's boathouse. The paint was drying, I was checking for fissures—close enough to inhale the colors. Splendor savored in variance to Mirth and Mirth to Good Cheer. I painted for fifty years, but I'd never noticed that there's a dissimilarity in the breath of the pigments in the air, red being very tart, blue middling, and yellow, of all things, mild."

"You died breathing red?" Jimi asked.

"Violet," she said. "Ultraviolet, rather."

"I know that chord," he said.

"Pardon me?"

"That chord. It's all the same spectrum, music and color. I could never play it, but I heard it all the time in my dreams. Do you ever have dreams where you're underwater?"

"Yes, I've done some leviathans, sirens, and River Gods. Quite a few River Gods."

"Whaddya know?" he smiled. "So, where we going?"

She tilted her head and the braids danced at either blade of her jaw. The toes of her right foot flexed in her bronze moccasin. She looked like a child with a giddy secret.

"C'mon, you can trust me," he said.

"I'm only an emissary, Mr. Hendrix, but I can't trust you because you never trusted you. You didn't trust your whereabouts, let alone your destination."

"How will I know where I'm going?"

"You'll know when you get there."

"How?"

Jimi gave her the full wattage, a flare in his teeth to light the fount of her heart. The corner of her mouth sagged, the lock on the secret giving in to gravitational pull.

"There's a place called 'Schwarzchildland,' and in it a smaller place called 'Red City.' You'll know when you're there because it will be dark and red."

"Is it far?"

"It's three exits from here. The one marked 'Abandon.' Suffice?"

"I guess."

"Good. Now, wash up."

He looked into the bowl and, only for an instant, the tone of the water turned to a crepuscular rainbow—four bands of pink, two of coarse blue, one of lusterless white approaching gray, the rose motionless in the center.

---

Chevron could enter the Louvre via Pangaea Online and even penetrate the storage catacombs and the underground vaults (where once there were armaments, there was now disused art). She could access the paranoia of a dead crown while learning of a history removed from time, a history more tactile than time, a history of awe, and there was the sensation of déjà vu even then, though her life was only ten and eleven years long, and though this was some years before the illness and the panoply of medicines with their theater of side effects. In the dropsical Flemish portraiture, the children with the vapid eyes and the even more vapid countenances of marine life, she recognized aquanauts, goldfish kids such as herself, treading water, buffeted in place while waves of confusion, riot, and development crested all around them. This oceanic feeling was present before the epilepsy, and at its advent she thought of the sickness as God's own antidote, God's own redeeming plague. Of course, how fitting, thank you so very much, she couldn't help but think as she drifted to the overhanging plaster and watched the somnambulistic emergency drill, the ninth graders closing their circle, the homeroom teacher coming forward with cat's strides, holding the stub of a pencil. Finally, when she dared to look, she saw herself convulsing on the floor like a voudon celebrant with her white satin panties gleaming, an imbecile's smile on her face, and her palms stretched in supplication as though praying to her better self on the ceiling.

Since the age of twelve, Chevron had kept a journal that

evolved, quickly, into a book of quotations, hers alone. Following the seizure, she wrote, "Prayers are not generally answered but replied to, and very often they are contested." Certitude quickly took on the capricious nature of prayer since the illness dispelled neither her isolation nor her omnipotence. Children shunned her for fear of contamination, and her own mother and father interacted with her as though she were an unbroken and quite possibly rabid, albeit exotic, house pet, to be indulged but never loved. They papered her room with expensive reproductions of the melancholic eighteenth-century Bolognese painter Donato Creti, whom she'd taken something of a liking to, and plied her with Biber and Hendrix discs. They served her sweet tea, vitamins, and prescription drugs that left her giddy and sleepless, and talked to her of the futility of dressing and going outside. She passed this attitude onto the moon as she brooded away the nights on the window's ledge, her bare feet dangling, playing on the harp of air. She would tell the moon to its face that it was but an "uncultured pearl before swine."

Henrich Ignaz Franz von Biber's work was a religion she imbibed in lieu of slumber. His *Rosary Sonatas* were prayer for prayer's sake, worshipping only their form of address and willing nothing but their own will. Biber was the tonic to Hendrix, and Hendrix was circular road music, guileless thunder and metamorphosis, a flaming cloverleaf. Hendrix, it seemed, always ended up back where he had begun and always in a cloud of incandescence. He was precreation and Chevron was post. They were fire and water, antithetical elements that shared a common soul. Jimi left nothing unscathed, nothing unconverted, except for her, his soul-twin. Sadly, even fire would not put out the ocean. Her mother bought her a mixing board and she aired the music of his vocals—his "sweet daddy" monotone was a sop to the same vulgar element who put their leaden musket to the head of Amadeus and forced him to write his crowning Punch and Judy opera.

It was Hendrix who convinced her that the logical thing to do was to get out of the house on a regular basis, that there was a "slight return" to each journey and each of life's little autos-da-fé was a forging, a quickening of identity. She would hear nothing of her parents' arguments to the contrary; she was going to find employment that would swallow up the nights and it was going to be a road job, something in carting or livery. The Yellow Cab people gave her a map of a district across state lines and told her to study it, as though they were travel agents. The garbage Don on Alameda, a Mr. Di Nuccio, offered her a job transporting espresso in his social club for tips. He stressed that the experience would improve her interpersonal skills. The wits in the dispatch department at the Transit Authority were calling South Central "The Nam," and the tenured drivers would not have ridden in an armored caravan through the area. Her application was speed-processed when she told the managers how the exhale of the city bus's air brakes, hours before dawn, was like the nightingale to her ear.

She arrived to find the South Central nights a victim of their own reputation—desolate, yes, but more as a result of crime prevention than crime itself. There was random target practice going on, and indeed there were art Turks who would venture out nightly to prove that the shattering of glass was a legitimate form of self-expression. However, as Chevron knew, home and auto vigilantism were the true tyrants of these streets. Innocent passersby were outlined in sodium vapor beams from front porches and dashboards, and disembodied and guttural biker voices resounded in Dolby, "Go for yours, fungoid!" or "Let's see what you got besides a yeast infection!"

The few passengers she did get were in no hurry to reach the enigma of where they were going. She soon realized that many of them were, like her, along for the ride, though the only ones who showed any interest in the scenery were the infants, shackled in their strollers in the alcoves she created by folding the handicapped isles into the wall. The music on the boom panel at her feet was hardly ever remarked upon. She indulged her passengers their smoking, spitting, and lying down and they conceded Chevron her religion. Some of them even hummed along, well, not along. Those premature mothers with only a slightly edgier cast of scrutiny in their eyes than prom girls, and those stick-limbed sentinels with their perfume bottle pipes, yes, humming softly in counterpoint as though Jimi's guitar was slowly and deliberately electrocuting them. Some of them bongoed the seats, some reveled in the lyric "You say that it's okay / You just want me to take you for a ride," and some wanted to send "All Along the Watchtower" out to all the brothers in Soledad, and "Red House" out to all the brothers selling plasma.

When sleep did return to Chevron, it assimilated its way into her routine like a gracious houseguest and it brought no loss of motor function. She would forego a stop here and there, a wa-wa effect, an aside from the Hammond B3 organ, "Night Bird Flying" would segue unaccountably into "In from the Storm," and no one ever called her on it but for one old queen with glitter makeup and a snuff tin who went by the name "Glam I Am." Glam, on the hilly route along Central, told her, "You mind those slopes, sugar. Goin' up ain't comin' down and likewise in reverse."

She took to chain-popping No Doze, figuring that the pharmaceutical dispute inside her could not get any more volatile. She soon found herself a neurotic sleepwalker, her new speech patterns putting her in mind of a jazzed, avant-garde raga, the largo hard on the heels of the allegro. She was something of a musician at last, but still narcoleptic and perfectly capable of getting a complete nap between the alveolar of "Take" and the bilabial of "your belongings." Determined, she began sipping Peruvian espresso through the tube of a thermos big as an air tank and blowing caustic, noisome air bubbles into the bowl when her stomach would brook no more coffee. Curfewed children, chain-linked saffron blurs behind the windows of their public housing units, registered her pizzicato driving method and shouted for Chevron to "Take it the fuck out of first!"

At the end of her route—not fifty yards from the terminal—was the newly restored Gretchen Dankmur Vesperbild-designed State Sanitarium. It had a lustrous façade, a vast reception area, a cafeteria facility, and an opera hall, all on the lobby level, and parfait tiers of pillowed berths and electrode labs above, rising into the clouds. It was not as though the idea had never lasered through her mind, since the bus was always empty when the sanitarium rolled into view. Even the structure's shadow was thought to be a harbinger of ill luck. Chevron herself hated the sight of the building with the refined venom of the bullied, its very existence giving the lie to her triumph over her own particular challenge. She was certain that she was "conscious" when the sanitarium issued its magnetic summons, but whether or not she was waking or sleeping was a matter that even the autopsy equivocated. The fact was that the memories—the front wheels humping up over the curve, the top F clarion from a siren on high, the synth nebula where Jimi had formerly spoken, "Hey, a golden wing ship is passing my way," the hale shower, and the sad, sleepy sigh of the building's main staves—would have seemed like dream stills in any case.

---

The neon said, "Abandon," in liquid color, not unlike the texture of a campfire, but down the ramp Jimi found the atmosphere of Schwarzchildland almost cheering. There were endless quotients carved into the stone corridors, obviously taken verbatim from some encyclopedic mathematical primer. There were monarch moths of black, white, and amber sizzling in the air—he would stroke the bus's grill when they arrived and extract a handful of winged pirate's treasure—and the sight of the naked guardsmen patrolling the rampway with sharpened trowels triggered a vague *National Geographic* recollection of the Masai with their pipework bodies, capacious heads, and truculent dignity.

Jimi waved and got a show of teeth in response, the very few that they had left. He noticed that his breath wasn't fogging the window. Indeed, he was not breathing—that's right!—and upon further investigation he was reminded that his heartbeat had been postponed as well. He turned from the window in stages, seeing himself in his mind's eye, a jerky flipbook show. Lady

Creti would have stood ten feet tall if she were inclined to rise, and as it was, her legs formed a collapsed drawbridge in the aisle.

"How . . . tall . . . am . . . I?" Jimi asked, afraid to look at his own legs, the fragment taking forever in the air, something like a nonagenarian mute's first words ever. Her face had elongated into a feral African mask, and as she answered he saw a sequence of drowsy photos of an animated totem.

"You . . . are . . . a . . . legend."

"Huh?"

"Listen."

Far in the distance, a lone grasshopper faintly solicited for company and recreation and shortly hundreds more answered the call in such sweet attunement that Jimi was convinced that this vast string section was charged with learning but a single melody—perfectly. The danger was in having hollow spaces around perpetuum mobiles. How many times had he swelled Mitch Mitchell's drumheads into rounded pans of over-yeasted bread and he remembered way back, all-day practice in roadside lodges, the varnish flaking off the inside of the bureau drawers and those tenant roaches dead with their lacy bellies propped up. The stomachache faded in as the music grew louder. Jimi smelled seafood on his own breath. He glanced at Lady Creti and saw a painless vapor leaking from her mouth.

The scenery had been monochromatic since they entered onto the ramp, but now ahead loomed a red haze—a casino's neon in a fog—its spectrum passing from high pink through flame-red, and ultimately into a luminous hysteria that had his eyes watering. He closed them, but his pupils burned in the dark. Opening his eyes, he saw that he had wept scorched tears onto the front of his winding sheet. The bus ground to a halt, the string section played on, the miasma so thick now that, stomachache and all, he wanted Lady Creti right there on the floor of the bus. He wanted to take her in the brume of a volcano, and wanted a second chance at life so that he could die again doing it.

"Mother Biber will see you now," she said, smiling.

Coming through the abbey, the music loud in his ears, he recalled his one regret—he could never get that glassy Amati tone from a guitar. He'd tried bowing with Indian-head coins and Yale keys and failed on both attempts, and thus had to grant autonomy to Moog specialists who were nothing but glorified engineers. It wasn't only the music that reminded him; each surface of the abbey's interior was reflective, the Mother Abbess's taste for icy furnishings extending to the divans, the buffets, and the crystalline staircases that featured steps as curved and unnavigable as a swan's back, leading up to nothing. Farther on, the steam began to rise from the tiles. Jimi hotfooted his way down the corridor, solely for the sake of his own entertainment. His feet were mitten-numb although his bellyache was holding; he was hunting the source of the music from foggy room to foggy room. The acoustics of the cloisters were intentionally deceptive, Jimi knew, the mysterious prayers of the sisters meant to ask only that the Almighty begin His movements in His mysterious ways. The nuns were in the end but furtive yodelers daring an avalanche. A black girl in a stained toga with a high, prickly Afro bound with a blue sash stood in a random doorway. Her pupils were stretched into dual question marks.

"What's your name?" the two of them asked in tandem. Then "You first," and "No, yours." She won his heart on the spot because Jimi, sulky around women, particularly after he'd bedded them, always longed for a companion who could read and interpret his thoughts quicker than he could, as his stratocasters were apt to do. He extended his hand and she hers and they shook hands in a jailhouse, her touch as cool and aristocratic as the feel of a chalice. Jimi listened hard this time to make sure her response held no guesswork.

"I'm going to find the Mother Superior and ransom you with my very soul," the two of them said together.

---

Mother Biber sat behind her rampart desk, regarding Jimi in the entryway. Her chin lay astride the womb of her Jacob Stainer. Jimi knew now why he heard an entire chamber orchestra in the air: Mother Biber's bow was having insouciant sex with the strings, and in the very act one heard the mellifluousness of generations to come. She stopped playing and a siren of protest went off in his ears. Her features were expansively sculpted in the Teutonic manner—only the lips purposely left wanting as though to suggest, amid the contrast, that cruelty was indeed only a reduction, only an absence. She laid the bow down on the desk and it burned into the wood. A white vine rose in the air between the two of them. She opened the single drawer, spacious as a meat rack, and drew forth a foaming stein.

"Come have a bromide, Jimi," she said.

He took the cup and blew into it, the foam every which way. She read his hesitation.

"You're already . . ." she said.

He drank and found that there was nothing liquid in the cup—it was a mug of hot suds. His bellyache died on the vine.

"Sit."

Jimi stooped into a rounded chair. It was shallow from the floor and slatted at the sides as though fashioned from a small barrel.

"Who's the tall sister down the hall?" he said.

"Who?"

"I'm asking you. The tall black girl in the white mini with the Mandingo 'do?"

"I see. You know, the greatest misconception among newcomers is that they have somehow landed in a pot of primulas. We do encounter difficulties here and sometimes we are forced to make concessions to parallel universes. Often up is down, black is white, and life here has a certain looking-glass logic. It's the equivalent of statecraft or diplomacy in the world. In time, everything will become clear."

"That's what they say in the world."

"They'll say anything in the world. That's what I wanted to discuss with you."

"I'm confused."

"Jimi, stop fighting it," Mother Biber said. "Confusion is a form of resistance, a kind of denial."

"Fine, let's get on with it."

"And don't be impatient. That's another form of denial."

"Well, what do you want me to say?"

"I want you to listen. I want you to empty your mind of all thoughts. I want you to let them pour like vapor through your nostrils."

"Sure," Jimi said and clamped his eyes shut.

"Make a barren prairie of your mind."

"Done."

"Is it quiet in your mind?"

"It's . . ."

"Yes?"

"It's all air."

"But do you hear the current?"

Jimi cracked his eye and Mother Biber leaned across the desk and jolted his lid closed with a cobalt beam.

"The current?" Jimi asked

"The sloshing of the cerebrospinal fluid. Do you hear it?"

"I feel it more than hear it. It's like my brain vaguely has to pee."

"Then pee vaguely."

"Okay."

"Hear it now?"

"Oh, yeah."

"Good. That is the sound of time at low tide," Mother Biber said.

"It's like a little winter wind."

"Oh, yes. And in the center of that small howling, there's . . . ?"

"A whistling."

"Yes. No. It's not a whistling but another sort of manipulation of air. This is the sound of sul ponticello—the violin at full mast. It's a note low enough for the ear to hear but too high to perceive in toto. That's the vamp of eternity, Jimi. Before I died, I wrote a requiem mass. For a man. I thought it quite beautiful, the last little laurel leaf of forty years of composition. But, in the world, the discernment of beauty is predicated on its ephemerality. In the world, nothing durable and open-ended can be beautiful. They want only their roses, you see, their youth, and their twilight. They want their doomed and foolhardy negations of time. Imagine what a requiem mass not for man but for all of time would sound like? Or perhaps I shouldn't ask you to imagine it. Perhaps you are hearing it. That first note, Jimi. So . . . so . . . sustained."

Jimi labored to open his eyes and from across the great plank Mother Biber saw a sleeper struggling to read a clock face.

"That doesn't make sense. You can't write a requiem mass for time because time is not dead."

Mother Biber said, "Yes, but we are," and then added, "Isn't it grand?" as she opened the single drawer again and pushed a deck of tarots, bound with a strip of vermilion-colored lace, across the desk.

"We'll write the requiem together, maestro. I'd like it to be fugual in structure. Subject, antecedent, consequent. Past, present, and future. But do you know what? You're going to have to put your thoughts back in your mind now. It's time for my favorite program."

He wanted to ask what deep root, what earthen stovepipe she'd heard his music blaring out of, but the Abbess read an alternate question in his reddened eyes. She answered the question by saying, "Judges One, Three, Live!"

"What?" Jimi asked.

And God's own interrogation lamp blazed overhead. She turned to the light, put her fist over her ear, and announced, "Come up with me into my lot, that we may fight against the Canaanites, and likewise I will go with thee into thy lot."

There was a cawing somewhere close at hand and she told him to answer the phone. He searched the desktop and found only a blushing seashell. He put the pod to his ear.

A voice said, "Hi, this is Bob from Fortezza County."

"Hi, Bob."

"Listen, a mental patient—Russian émigré, mid-thirties, did his own hair—came in yesterday on a violation of a writ of restraint. His mother's, actually. He was found asleep in her basement and that's where it gets sticky. It was her summer home and she's currently not in residence there. The caretaker found him. Any half-decent defense attorney would just slap that one back up the ice at us. I had to order a D.P., that's Decline Prosecution. Then, hours later, he's out by my car, just standin' there with his hands in his pockets. I might have asked him if he wanted a lift."

Jimi had the tarot deck open and was rifling through it. There were dignitaries of the wand, the cup, the sword, the pentacle, as well as pictorials of the sun, the reaper, Satan, and the hanged man. He finally managed to deal himself a suite, using the tree swinger as the keynote.

"You drive a hack in your spare time, Bob?"

"Hell, no."

"Was there a question?"

"Well, obviously I'd like to know if fate will hold it against me. My hand was forced, but that's one more lost child out in the open with my signature on his release papers."

Jimi looked at the cards.

"Bob, he'll be back."

"Why, sure he will."

"When you see him again, I'd like you to throw the library at him."

"How'm I gonna do that?"

"Sentence him to Disneyland."

"What the hell did you say?"

"Sentence him to Disneyland and appoint yourself chaperone."

"I would be removed from the bench."

"All right then, Bob, drill a hole in your head, reach your hand in, and take out your conscience. Aloha."

With an almost imperceptible motion of his arm, he hung up the shell and returned it to his ear. A crank said, "And a one-a and a two-a" and then began to sing to the tune of "Heartbreak Hotel": "Well, since my life has left me / I found a new way to swell / I'm a natural gas below the grass / I call that H-E-L-L."

Jimi terminated the call and assured the viewing audience that there was no reason to worry. Over at the Home they were only allowed one outgoing phone call per resident on a nightly basis.

"Next," Jimi said into the carapace.

The connection was fraught with static. It was as though whoever it was on the other end was calling in from the region of recovered memory.

"Hi, this is Chevron from a cell in The Nam."

Jimi played along. "What could I do for you, Chevy?"

"I'm gonna run it aground up against the State Sanitarium over by the bus terminal. Take a few of mine with me."

"You want the hari-kari hotline."

"I want you, brother."

He dealt himself a new suite.

"Bud," he said, "I see real problems with this. You really want to wait until a new moon in a date that coincides with threes in each bracket."

"I don't have time for that."

Jimi looked at Mother Biber. "Forgive them for all they think they know," he said.

"What?" said Chevron.

"Never you mind, buddy. You do what you have to do."

He scanned the suite for the Death card. To his surprise, it was a nativity scene, a Nordic illumination. It was Caravaggesque in its use of lamplight, but much sweeter and lacking the southerner's foreboding pall. The faces of the cherubs, and even the face of the Christ child, were so stout and serene as to suggest Down's syndrome, and the face of the Madonna was tranquil and piggish as well. The setting was not a manger at all, but unmistakably a marble crypt—a rent in the ceiling revealed the apses of a neighboring cathedral. The placid Savior lay with his feet crossed and his palms open and supplicant. He was looking up at Joseph, or was it a stray from the wise trinity who stood with his back to the viewer, his locks tight and simmering like a cropped Afro and his robe so rumpled and fiery-red that Jimi thought it could only be a magic carpet? Previous to visiting Red City, he would have wondered what the illustration had to do with death.

"A long time ago I saw you in the Louvre," Chevron said.

"Saw me in the Louvre? I've been on that block but never inside."

"But still. You were visiting Jesus on his birth bed."

"Was I one of the wise?" Jimi asked.

"No, you were one of the mad."

"Well, what was a madman doing with baby Jesus?"

"It looked to me like you were about to fly."

He hung up and the klieg light blinked out. Jimi and the Abbess sat in the dark with the shell glowing on the table between them.

"Someone is homesick," Jimi said.

"Your home is here now."

"I don't know if I meant me."

"Hmm?"

"I think this seashell wants to go back in the sea."

"It isn't that simple. You came here to help me write the requiem. It's what you died for."

"You got any water around here?"

"A baptismal Jacuzzi in the back."

"Won't do. Am I your prisoner?"

"Well . . . no."

"You said time was at low tide here, Mother. How hard could it be for you to wait?"

Mother Biber said, "You'd have to live a hundred thousand lifetimes to return."

"Oh, yeah?" said Jimi. "And how many deaths would I die?"

"Perhaps, if you return," she said, "you will be the one to tell me."

She fumbled in the darkness for her violin and her bow. In the doorway, Jimi heard the very same air that she was playing when he came in. Only it was played backward.

---

Chevron is at the wheel and Jimi is back in his handicapped rumble seat with a quill pen and a scroll the size of a pillar. To this day, he hasn't learned musical notation, so he writes his requiem mass out phonetically. It begins, "Waaa-wooo-weee-awww . . ." They have seen primordial lava and Jimi's stood up next to a thousand mountains, but as yet they've had no glimpse of the seashore. They inspired the wheel in southern Mesopotamia and a stopover in Troy gave rise to a legend of a horse. Jimi leans out the window and drinks the air, finds it dry, and spits it out. Late at night, Chevron calls in to dispatch and prays for a blue tomorrow. The bus stalks the sea. The life that they've lived is dead.

## The Flannery O'Connor Award for Short Fiction

David Walton, *Evening Out*

Leigh Allison Wilson, *From the Bottom Up*

Sandra Thompson, *Close-Ups*

Susan Neville, *The Invention of Flight*

Mary Hood, *How Far She Went*

François Camoin, *Why Men Are Afraid of Women*

Molly Giles, *Rough Translations*

Daniel Curley, *Living with Snakes*

Peter Meinke, *The Piano Tuner*

Tony Ardizzone, *The Evening News*

Salvatore La Puma, *The Boys of Bensonhurst*

Melissa Pritchard, *Spirit Seizures*

Philip F. Deaver, *Silent Retreats*

Gail Galloway Adams, *The Purchase of Order*

Carole L. Glickfeld, *Useful Gifts*

Antonya Nelson, *The Expendables*

Nancy Zafris, *The People I Know*

Debra Monroe, *The Source of Trouble*

Robert H. Abel, *Ghost Traps*

T. M. McNally, *Low Flying Aircraft*

Alfred DePew, *The Melancholy of Departure*

Dennis Hathaway, *The Consequences of Desire*